ORION

ISBN 978-0-578-00595-9

Contact: mdberman@verizon.net

Manufactured in the United States of America

For Tara and Noah

Chapter 1.   KANSAS CITY, MISSOURI

Maybe you've heard that an alien abduction is a real spectacular affair, involving flashing, rainbow colored lights and an explosion of sound worthy of the movies. Or maybe you've heard the opposite, that it's a secret, clandestine operation, occurring in the middle of the night, with the E.T.'s yanking the human abductee right out of his or her bed. Well, allow me to set the record straight. It's both. Or at least, in my case it was both, a combination of stealth and spectacle.

I'll get into the details of my abduction in a moment, but for right now, I just want to clearly state the purpose of this journal — this is a complete and total account of my experiences with extraterrestrials, from the time I was abducted on June 7th, 2008, to the time I was returned to Earth, on June 9th, 2008, exactly two days later. I've chosen to write down the details of my travels in this format because it allows for the most elaboration, and it's very important that you hear every single thing I have to say about beings that live in outer space.

If I sound a little urgent or dramatic, it's not on purpose. Maybe it will help you to know I didn't always used to talk this way. I used to talk just like all the other kids I know. But since my alien abduction, I've begun to talk a bit differently. I know bigger words now, and bigger thoughts. And when I mix them with my normal, modern-day, teenage vocabulary, it unintentionally comes off a bit sophisticated. You see, there I go again. But I have to use these kinds of words if I'm ever going to get my story across to adults... and they're the ones who are going to have the hardest time believing it.

Now, in order for you to fully understand where this account is headed, I need to explain a little bit about where I'm from. I was born in 1995 to Derek and Karen Albright of Kansas City, Missouri. Life in our hometown was idyllic and peaceful, the perfect picture of middle America. Sure, it could be a little boring, but it was stable and I liked it. I imagined living there happily ever after and becoming a farmer just like my dad.

My dad took farming pretty seriously, and in order to keep up on all the latest advances in the industry, he used to visit farmers in towns all across America, learning about the newest techniques and innovations. Whenever he came home, he'd invariably bring some agricultural sample with him, like pieces of rock, bags of dirt, or glass jars filled with colored sand that he'd give to Katie and me as presents. Oh, right, Katie — she's my little sister, and she has a very important role in all this. But her part doesn't come into play until much later in the story, so for the time being, there won't be much mention of her, except to say that she's 4 years younger than me and has the capacity to be either infinitely annoying or infinitely cool, depending on what side of the bed she wakes up on.

"These are from far away cities," my dad would say, tossing out the names of towns I'd never heard of, like Calypso, Janus, or Pandora.

Over the years, the odd assortment of dirt samples piled up, basically turning my room into a Geology museum. And while I admit there was a part of me that thought my dad's obsession with the Earth was pretty cool, there was another part of me that wished he wasn't so, well, eccentric.

My dad's also a fantastic storyteller, and most nights after our family dinner, we'd all sit out on the porch and he'd spin tales about everything under the sun, literally. He knew all the stars, planets and constellations and loved to point them out to Katie and me. I never really saw the "Bull" that was supposed to be Taurus, or the "Warrior" that was supposed to be Orion. I just saw a bunch of random stars. But still, it was fun listening to my dad explain all the ancient myths behind them.

Occasionally, he'd even launch into a science-fiction tale, something about aliens from other worlds, and these would inevitably be my favorite stories. The best part was my dad would never admit he was making them up. He'd tease me and claim that aliens were real, and that there was a whole secret universe of intelligent life up in outer space that nobody on Earth knew about. "Sometimes the truth is stranger than fiction," he used to say. I thought he was being playful with me, and I loved him for it.

As you can probably tell, I was happy growing up in Kansas City and I would have been content for everything to stay just the way it was. However, about one year ago, just after I finished 6th grade, my parents suddenly and mysteriously disappeared.

I didn't even learn what happened to them until the day after it happened. My parents had gone away to visit my aunt and uncle in Des Moines, Iowa. They secured my grandparents as babysitters for the weekend, a move that completely irritated me since I thought I could've handled the job myself. I begged them to let us stay home alone, but my pleas fell on deaf ears. They were taking a 200 mile road trip and three days was simply too long a time to be left 'unsupervised', as my parents put it. Now don't get me wrong, I love spending time with my grandparents, I just felt like I deserved a little more trust than that.

Anyway, on the last day of their trip, Sunday, July 15th, 2007, we were all gathered around the dinner table waiting for them to come home. They were due in at six, but when nine o'clock rolled around and they still weren't home and they hadn't called and they weren't answering their cell phones, things started to feel a little weird.

Finally, at around 10 o'clock, a pair of headlights pulled up the dirt road to our farm and a wave of relief flooded over me. But that relief changed to confusion when I realized it wasn't my parents. It was a police car. It came to a stop beside the front porch and a uniformed policeman emerged, striding up our path. My grandfather rose to meet him at the door.

"Can I help you?"

"I'm looking for the family of Derek and Karen Albright," said the officer.

"I'm their father," said my granddad.

"May I come in?"

A chill went through me as my grandfather opened

the screen door. It was strange to see a policeman walk right into our house. He was young, with a trim haircut and a serious face. He noticed me and Katie and shot my grandparents a look.

"Alan, Katie, would you two go upstairs to your rooms, please?" said my grandfather.

I had no intention of missing what was about to be discussed, but I wasn't about to put up an argument either. So instead, Katie and I left the room and went upstairs, then I turned right and faked going into my room, then I waited until she actually went into hers, and then I tip-toed back downstairs and crouched low just outside the sliding pocket door to the kitchen. I heard muffled voices on the other side but couldn't make out what anyone was saying. Ever so carefully, I slipped my fingers into the crack between the wall and the door and slid it open just a few inches. As I pressed my face into the gap, I could see my grandparents seated at the kitchen table with the policeman. My grandfather looked confused.

"But it doesn't make sense," he was saying. "If there are no bodies—"

"It happens, Mr. Edwards," said the policeman. "A vehicle goes over the bridge, hits the water, the impact causes the windows to shatter and the bodies float out. They get caught in the current and drift downstream..."

"So you go further down, and you set up checkpoints," said my grandfather.

"We've done that, Sir. Don't get me wrong, we're not giving up the search. I'm just here to advise you of the situation, and let you know the reality."

The policeman paused.

"In all probability, your daughter and her husband have drowned."

I gasped.

Everyone in the room turned suddenly and caught sight of me. Slowly, I opened the door.

"Alan, go back to your room," said my granddad.

"What's happening?" I said.

My grandfather studied me for a long moment. Then he walked over and kneeled down to my eye level.

"We don't know anything for certain," he said. "But... there was a car accident... and your parents' truck went over a bridge, into the Missouri. The police found the car, but they haven't found mom and dad yet."

The policeman stood there, then nodded goodbye.

"We're doing everything we can," he said. "We're not giving up hope."

He placed his card on the table and turned to go. As he pushed through the screen door and walked out onto the porch, for some strange reason, I followed him. I watched the officer climb back into his car and drive off. It felt like he was my only link to my parents, and as the police cruiser pulled away, my knees suddenly gave way and I sat down on the porch in a state of shock.

*   *   *   *   *

Luckily, as I would learn by the time of this writing, the police didn't know the whole story, my parents didn't get into any car accident and they certainly didn't drown in the missouri river. And although technically speaking I couldn't have known that at the time, somehow, deep in my bones, I felt it. Maybe I was in denial, maybe I was just stubborn, but I flat-out refused to believe my parents were gone. I made it my mission to hold out hope as long as possible that they were still alive out there and I wouldn't talk to anyone who said otherwise — including my grandparents and Katie.

Of course it didn't matter what I felt. There were practical things to be dealt with. The state of Missouri issued death certificates for my parents and technically speaking, Katie and I became orphans. Our grandparents became our legal guardians and sold their house and moved into ours. They tried their best to return us to some semblance of a normal life, but honestly, it was impossible. I felt like I was acting.

When I started Junior High in the fall, my grades plummeted. For the first time ever I actually started failing a class and although it bothered me on some deep level, for the most part I just didn't care. School felt completely and utterly pointless.

On top of all that, the responsibility of operating the farm fell squarely on my shoulders. My grandfather handled the business end of things, but the manual labor was mostly left to me, and the workload became overwhelming. I mean, I'd always done my share of chores, but with my father gone, I had to step up and assume a million more duties. I became skilled at roping cattle, husking corn, collecting eggs and seeding the fields. My grandfather even taught me how to handle myself competently on the heavy machinery, including my dad's pride and joy, a John Deere hunter green 5025 series

tractor. Basically, I began running the farm and although
that took my mind off my parents a little, it also wound up
making me dog tired, all the time. Combine that with my
general lack of interest in my schoolwork and I started the
bad habit of falling asleep in my classes on a regular basis.
I held on to the belief that my parents were still alive
somewhere and my life was just a bad dream from which,
if I kept sleeping, one day I'd wake up.

    Finally, I did get a wakeup call. It was a few months
after my parents' accident and I was having a great
daydream. I mean, the kind of nap you can only have in the
middle of the day, with the birds chirping outside the
window. The only problem was, this nap was taking place
in the middle of Mrs. Peachtree's 5th period English class.
And although I had been doing this on a consistent basis
for the last 6 weeks, this time, from stories I heard, was
by far my biggest offense. I had snored, yawned, drooled,
and even muttered out loud a few times, although,
thankfully, what I said was apparently unintelligible. My
teacher, Mrs. Peachtree, is a very cool lady and the fact
that this happened in the middle of her class makes it all
the more embarrassing. I liked her and I thought she liked
me. But after this incident, I've never really been sure.

    You see, Mrs. Peachtree couldn't wake me up. I mean,

apparently, she'd tried everything — the ruler-smacking-the-desk bit, banging erasers over my ears, and even slapping me on the back with her palm. But I just kept on sleeping, and the class thought it was hysterical. Brandon Berman was firing spitballs at me, hitting me dead on, but I was oblivious. Andy Weiner, my best friend and a class clown in his own right, was whispering my name, trying to save me from getting my first detention, but I was deaf to it. And Kevin McCain even threw a book at me — but I just kept snoozing. (All of this I was informed of and reminded of every day for a week afterwards).

So do you know what Mrs. Peachtree finally did? When the bell rang, she dismissed the class, locked the classroom door and then just left me there. And I kept on dreaming, in what some kids now refer to as "The Great Snooze of '07", missing 6th period up 'til 9th. When the final school bell started ringing, I remember specifically having a dream that I was missing all my classes... and so I finally opened my eyes.

I had drooled all over the desk and my shirtsleeve. I looked up, bleary-eyed, to see my grandparents, Mrs. Peachtree, and the principal of the school, Doug Carter, standing above me. Mr. Carter was bald with glasses, a lean build, and tried to look young and cool, wearing jeans and sweaters. He had his arms folded across his chest.

"Having a good dream, Albright?" he said.

I stayed silent, trying to collect my whereabouts.

"Let me ask you something, I'm just curious... do you think it's cool to fall asleep on a teacher?" he continued.

"No," I said.

I guess he didn't expect me to answer so quickly, because he just ignored it and kept on with his prepared speech.

"When she's standing up here, giving you information that you're going to need in your life — do you think it's funny to pretend it's meaningless to you?"

Principal Carter never had much sympathy for me regarding the situation with my parents, and I didn't blame him. I didn't want sympathy. I wanted to be treated like everyone else.

"No... I'm really sorry, Mrs. Peachtree," I said.

"Alan, I know you've been through a lot, with your parents and everything," she said.

"Don't," I said. "I messed up and I know it, Mrs. Peachtree. I deserve detention."

"No, Alan," said Principal Carter. "This isn't just about today. This is about all the classes you've fallen asleep in this year, all the times you've been warned, but then continued to flaunt your disregard for the rules of our school. I'm sorry, son... this is a suspension."

My heart sank into my belly.

"Suspended?" I said. "For this?"

"Alan, we feel that you've reached a point where you think anything goes. We're here to tell you that, no, there are rules, and you can't break them, no matter how bad a hand you're dealt."

"This has nothing to do with my parents, Principal Carter. So could you please stop bringing them up?" I said.

"You really think this isn't about your parents' death—"

"They're not dead!" I said.

"That's enough," said my grandfather, stepping forward. "The punishment's been determined and we're standing by the principal."

"Grandpa... a suspension will ruin my school record. Mrs. Peachtree, I'm sorry," I said. I was begging now, but I couldn't stop myself. "I'll do anything."

"Alan, I believe in you, you know that," she said. "I

think you're a smart kid. At times, you even display flashes of real creativity. But if you don't break out of this slump—"

"I will. I'll try," I said. And then, and I'm so annoyed this happened because it caught me completely off guard, I started to cry. I guess my tears were enough to convince them to take pity, because Mrs. Peachtree finally sighed.

"Principal Carter — maybe there's another arrangement we can make. On weekends, as you know, I run the literacy program out of the school library. If Alan agrees to meet me there, every Saturday, and become a tutor, I think we can withdraw the suspension."

I was taken back. I mean, I'd been prepared to agree to anything. But this sounded like serious work. It wasn't just a commitment to a task, I realized, it was a commitment to 'something'. And I think that's exactly what Mrs. Peachtree wanted from me.

"I'll do it," I finally said.

Even Principal Doug Carter wasn't going to argue with this. He nodded, and my grandmother and I both let out sighs of relief.

To this day, I credit Mrs. Peachtree with helping me keep my grades — and my life — on track. I started to really turn things around over the next month, and although I wasn't knocking them out of the park, I started to get my grades up to passing, and that kept everybody happy.

In the meantime, there was still a part of me that refused to accept that my parents were gone. And although I stopped saying it to everyone else, secretly I began to investigate the details surrounding the accident. I bombarded the police station with phone calls, pressing the detectives for facts and evidence until I had compiled my own little case-file. The cops were sympathetic to me at first and offered up bits of information, but after awhile, I think they just found my questions annoying and stopped taking my calls, telling me they'd contact me if anything came up.

As I got more and more desperate with my investigation, I even began snooping around our house. I'm not proud of it, but whenever my grandparents and Katie were out, which was seldom, I went room-to-room, searching our entire property for something, anything, that might shed light on my mom and dad's disappearance.

And that's how I made the startling discovery that would set the events of this journal into motion.

One night over Thanksgiving break, my grandparents

took Katie out to see some animated princess movie and so I decided to stay home and investigate our barn. It's a classic 3-story red-and-white one, where we keep our horses, Peanut Butter and Jelly. The first floor is covered with haystacks and has an indoor-outdoor chicken coop. The second floor is filled with all my father's farm tools. And the third floor is storage, where my mom kept a bunch of antique furniture that she always said was going to be worth a lot someday. My father had instructed us many times never to go up there. He said it was too dangerous and declared the 3rd floor of the barn off-limits. But on this night, I broke my father's request and climbed the rickety ladder to the attic.

What I found there wasn't too startling at first. It was a storage area that looked like it had remained unused for years, with boxes and furniture piled everywhere. It seemed perfectly normal, and I started to think I was wasting my time looking for clues here.

But then I noticed something concealed beneath a tarp. It was stationed in the corner and there was a long cord snaking out from the base, plugging into an electric socket in the wall. I walked over and tugged the sheet free. It dropped, revealing what looked like an air-traffic controller's desk. There was a long display screen, with a big hand-sized dial, an antennae and a microphone. It was a radio, obviously, but it didn't look like any radio I'd ever seen before. I pulled up a chair, figured out where the power button was, and turned the thing on.

There was a high-voltage hum. I grabbed the mic.

"Hello?" I said.

There was no response.

"This is Alan. From Kansas City," I said, adding, "Kansas City, Missouri, not Kansas City, Kansas. Anybody copy?"

Again, nobody said anything, but I didn't really care. I just kept talking into the bizarre device. I talked about who I was and where I was from and before I knew it I had killed twenty minutes just blabbering away about nothing to no one. And the weird thing was it felt really good.

And so the next night, when I was having trouble sleeping, I snuck out of the house and started playing with the futuristic radio again. The idea of sending my thoughts out over the airwaves was thrilling to me and in my imagination I became the host of a syndicated national radio show, "The Alan Albright Show". I gave my opinions on everything from movies and TV shows to school politics and what was the best cafeteria lunch. I even started getting into some personal things, like my feelings about the big topic being discussed around the house lately — whether or not to have a funeral service for my mom and dad.

"How ridiculous is that?" I said into the microphone. "It hasn't even been a year. Don't think I'm being overly emotional, I looked it up on the internet and in missing persons cases, most people wait at least a year to have a service. Sure, this isn't your typical case, but still... what would you do, if you were me?"

I almost expected to get some callers, or have a sidekick give some kind of commentary back to me. But when nobody did, that's when it hit me that this radio probably didn't even work and that in all likelihood, I was sitting in a barn talking to myself. And you know what? I think it was just what I needed. Since my parents' accident, I hadn't really opened up to anyone, not Katie, not my grandparents, not even Andy, my best friend. But with the radio, I finally had an outlet. Every few nights, all through seventh grade, I crept out to the barn and started making my broadcasts. It felt like writing in a diary, or a journal, a safe place where I could talk about anything or anybody I wanted.

After all, no one was listening.

Chapter 2.   MY ALIEN ABDUCTION

I didn't know it, but the preliminary work for my alien abduction had been going on for an entire day prior to the actual event. You might presume a "spacenapping" happens suddenly, like a ship scoops you up in the middle of the night; and while that's mostly true, it's not the whole story. The whole story is, they stalk us. Beings from outer-space usually know exactly who they're coming down to get and why they've chosen that person. Apparently, pulling off a successful abduction is a huge undertaking and they don't take any chances.

As for the 'why' of it all, different people are abducted for different reasons.   For example, if you have a specific expertise about a particular subject or situation, The Pleidians might come for you to perform brain-scans in order to obtain your knowledge. They're big on data. Or if you have some incredibly special genetic material, like Tiger Woods or some other awesome athlete, The Grays might scoop you up and take a DNA sample so they can use your genes in scientific experiments.

For me, it was a different story, one a lot less flattering.   In fact, when I first heard the reason for my alien abduction, I was a bit insulted. It turns out I was

basically taken as part of an intergalactic scavenger hunt.
And while I'd later come to have a much more significant
role in things, at first, the only reason I was taken was
because the alien boy who abducted me wanted to win a bet
with his friends.

*   *   *   *   *

On Friday, June 6th 2008, I woke up late for school,
which wasn't unusual for me at the end of a school year. I
always took an advance on my summer break state of mind,
and this year had been no exception. I was staying up later
and later and on this particular morning, I had actually
been awake until one a.m. the night before.

Exhausted, I fumbled for the snooze button on my
alarm clock and through half-shut eyelids, I caught sight of
the display — 7:55 am. That was really late. Fortunately, I
only had one week left of school and that was enough to
motivate me. I jumped out of bed and made up the minutes
by taking the fastest shower in recorded history and then
just throwing on a baseball cap.

Now, in order to get to my bus stop, I have to cut
through the forest behind our house, my standard morning
routine. Usually the woods are empty and quiet, peaceful.

But on this particular Friday morning, as I was running at breakneck speed to catch the bus in time, I could swear I wasn't alone. It was eerie. At least twice I thought I heard footsteps chasing to keep up with me.

I made the bus in seconds flat, exhausted, and collapsed into a seat beside my best friend, Andy Weiner. Andy is the funniest kid in school and basically leaves me to be the guy in the background, just laughing or staying quiet, which I prefer. It's a perfect match, and when I told him that I thought I heard footsteps behind me in the forest, he was cool enough to take me seriously. He said that it was probably squirrels because it was summertime and they act up when they get overheated, so there's a lot of activity in the forest. See, that's the thing with Andy, you never know if he's making stuff up or if he actually knows what he's talking about. I presumed he did and decided to drop the notion that I was being followed.

But then boom, again, during Geometry class, just as we were learning about Pythagoras' theorem, I felt eyes on me. I looked at the classroom door and caught the glimpse of a shadowy figure outside in the corridor. As I glanced up, the figure went dashing off. I shook my head, wondering why in the world someone would be staring at me. After a few minutes, I convinced myself that I was being paranoid.

*   *   *   *   *

The next day, Saturday, June 7th, I learned that I wasn't. It was Katie's ninth birthday party and she invited every kid in her class. And so by sundown, our quiet little farm was completely overrun by a dozen hyperactive 3rd graders amped up on cake and ice cream. My grandpa hired a rodeo clown for the night, which I thought was kind of lame but Katie and her friends seemed to like. He also brought Peanut Butter and Jelly out of the stables and gave all of the kids horseback rides, which was a big hit.

After the party, Katie insisted on opening every single one of her presents, even though all her friends had gone home. I thought she was milking the whole birthday thing, but I didn't mind since I got to ride her coattails and stay up just as late as she did.

When she finally removed the last piece of wrapping paper from the last gift, it was about eleven p.m. and I started to crash. I kissed my grandparents goodnight, wished Katie a happy birthday and then stumbled up to my room, falling onto the bed with all my clothes and shoes on. I was prepared to sleep for at least 10 good hours, and I couldn't wait.

And then I heard a noise. It was a soft rustling sound, like a footstep, and it was close. I immediately opened my eyes. I hadn't bothered to turn on my lights and so at first I couldn't see anything. But as my pupils adjusted to the darkness, I got the shock of my life: There was someone standing in my room, hidden in the shadows. It was a boy, about my height, remaining quietly still in the corner, like a black cardboard cutout, trying not to be seen.

"Hello?" I said.

The kid didn't answer me.

"Party's over you know," I said, assuming it was one of Katie's friends. "You should have gone home a long time ago."

Silence.

"You know it's almost midnight? Your parents are probably worried about you."

I was starting to get a little nervous. This kid looked a little big to be one of Katie's 3rd grade classmates.

"Alright, come on, what are you doing in my room?" I said. "Get outta here!"

He stayed quiet once again, and so I decided to yell for Katie. I opened my mouth and started shouting her name, only to realize after about five seconds that my voice wasn't working. I was just sitting there upright in bed, my jaw hanging wide open, no sound coming out.

I tried to stand up, but my legs and arms weren't working either. I was completely paralyzed. Suddenly, the boy rushed towards me and pulled me right out of bed, dragging me towards my window. He was definitely strong. As he leaned out into the chilly night air, I saw a brilliant flash of white light, and my heart practically stopped—

There, floating just outside my room, was an unidentified Flying Object.

You don't forget the first time you see a UFO. The image of the spaceship hovering outside my window was so spectacular, that for a moment I just stared at it, captivated. It was an orb, perfectly round, about the size of a volkswagen Beetle. It was golden, shiny and metallic all over, except for a large, glass window located smack dab in the center. I heard it vibrating with an immense amount of energy, creating an eerie humming sound, like a bug-light in summer.

Suddenly, my attention shifted to a person sitting in the front seat, at the controls of the ship. It looked like a teenage girl. She flipped a switch and the interior of the UFO lit up and then she turned and looked right at me. Now, I only saw her for a brief second, but as she gazed through my bedroom window, I saw the most beautiful face I had ever seen, in this or any other galaxy. Her eyes sparkled with moonlight, impossibly, set like jewels in her exquisitely framed face -- well, all right, maybe I should stop right there, maybe I'm getting carried away. Celeste is probably going to be embarrassed now when she reads this -- either that or she's going to come find me and kick my butt. Suffice it to say, she's really pretty. And for a young boy age 12 at the time, seeing that girl, in that spaceship, was enough to convince me that I was dreaming.

I only got a quick glimpse of her when she turned her head, focusing on the dashboard.

"We've got company," she said.

"Who?" said the boy.

Suddenly, the ship went speeding off.

"Celeste! Where are you going?"

The next thing I knew, the boy spun around and dragged me out my bedroom door.

Downstairs, Katie and Grandpa were both asleep, the two of them snuggled together in his oversized chair. Grandmom was still awake in her rocker, watching the World Series of Poker on ESPN. I noticed all of this from an odd angle, as my abductor carried me across the living room, right behind my family's backs. I struggled to scream the whole time, but still no sound came from my mouth.

The boy quietly tiptoed across the floor and proceeded through the kitchen, dragging me right out the back entrance of our house. Then, he shut the screen door and headed deep into one of our family's enormous cropfields. I think the fact that I couldn't move made it easier for him to carry me. I was totally helpless.

Once we were a good distance away from the house, the kid dropped me onto the ground and I finally got a better look at him. He was wearing a bright silver jumpsuit, and a helmet with a red visor over his eyes, revealing only the lower half of his face. Except for his clothing, he looked completely human. This is the boy I would come to know as Ari Centauri, my best friend in outer space.

"Take it easy, would ya?" he said. "I come in peace."

He turned his attention toward the sky.

"Where did she go?" he continued to himself. "She wouldn't just leave me like this. Would she?"

I wasn't sure if I should reply, but since I couldn't, I didn't.

"She might if she was in danger," he said, figuring

out all the different options. "Or if by hanging around, she'd be putting me in danger".

He started to walk in random circles through the cropfield, scanning the stars. Suddenly, he jammed his finger upward, pointing at the zenith of the sky.

"There she goes!" he shouted, waving. "Celeste!"

He started running around, like a kid chasing fireflies, craning his neck. Above us, I saw the glowing trail of the giant UFO, passing high overhead. The humming orange orb made a U-turn in mid-air and came circling back around. Then, with the speed of a meteor, it plummeted downward and hit the ground, rolling. It turned over and over, coming right at us, until finally stopping just inches from where we stood. The circular window in the center of the orb swung open, and a metal staircase lowered down.

Out walked Celeste, the beautiful 13-year old pilot of the ship. Wearing a tight, black leather outfit, with a utility belt fitted snugly around her waist, she sure didn't look like any of the girls in my school. In one athletic leap, she jumped down the last few steps of the ladder and hurried over to us.

"You better not have hurt him, Ari," she said.

She kneeled beside me and gently placed her hand under my head.

"Are you okay, Alan?"

She knew my name? How did she know my name? I tried to ask that very question, forgetting that my voice didn't work. She stared at me for a moment, confused.

"What did you do, Ari? Did you use a freeze-ray on him?"

"I had to. He was giving me trouble."

"Well turn it off, would you?"

"He'll scream," said Ari.

"No, he won't," said Celeste, facing me. "Right, Alan? I mean if we unfreeze you, you're not going to yell, are you? You'll be cool?"

She stared into my eyes and suddenly I realized I could move them, so I moved them up and down.

"Wait, you mean you will scream?" she asked.

I darted them left to right.

"You won't scream. Okay. Good. That's what I thought. Now unfreeze him and let's get out of here, Ari," she said.

"Mistake," said Ari.

He raised his arm and on his wrist I saw a

futuristic watch. He pointed his fingers at me and twirled a dial on the face of the watch and then a bright blue laser beam came shooting at me. I felt the muscles and vocal cords in my neck loosen up and suddenly I could talk again.

Thrilled to have my voice back, I suddenly did the one thing that in hindsight, I shouldn't have done. I screamed.

"Grandpa!"

"I knew it," said Ari. "You can't trust an Earthling!"

He aimed his watch at me again and tapped it twice. A blue laser hit me and my voice went dead, right in the middle of my shout.

"You idiot, you're gonna get us killed!" said Celeste, turning angry on me.

Once again, I felt myself being dragged off my feet and carted sideways, right up the stepladder and into the hub of the spaceship. The kids from outer space filed in behind me, slamming the glass window shut.

Celeste took her seat behind the wheel. Ari pushed me into a chair and locked a safety belt around my waist. Then he plopped down beside Celeste, utterly confused.

"Okay, you wanna tell me what's going on?" he said. "Why'd you leave me?"

"Someone's on to us. Probably the E.P.A.," said Celeste. "Just like I knew would happen!"

Ari craned his neck, peering out the windshield.

"Where are they? I don't see them."

"Check the radar. They're out there."

"How many ships exactly?" said Ari.

"Three," said Celeste, "We have to get off this planet, hyperspeed."

She turned around in her chair, shouting.

"You strapped in, Alan?"

I didn't, or rather, I couldn't, answer.

"Unfreeze him."

Ari looked back at me.

"I don't think that's such a good idea, sis. This kid doesn't let up."

"It's too dangerous to leave him frozen if we come under attack. It's not right."

"Fine," said Ari, aiming his watch at me. He tapped it twice and I had control of my body back. And I decided to use it. If they thought I was gonna go easily, wherever I was going, they were wrong. I unhooked my seatbelt in the reverse order of the way I saw Ari lock it, and before they

knew what was going on, I kicked open the circular glass
door and jumped out of the ship.

"I told you! Unbelievable!" shouted Ari.

My feet hit the grass and my legs started pumping.
I sprinted half way across the field. Suddenly, I looked
back over my shoulder and saw Ari standing in the
doorway of the ship. He raised his hand and twisted the
dial on his watch. The freeze-ray hit me again and I felt
my leg muscles tense up for a third time. I tipped over
and smacked hard to the ground. Ari came hurrying down
the ladder of the ship, kneeling beside me.

"Alan, take it easy. Okay? Look at me."

I stared up into his eyes.

"This isn't your typical alien abduction, okay? We're
not gonna scan your brain or probe your butt or anything.
This is gonna be fun."

If I had to trace my friendship with Ari back to a
particular moment, it would be right then. In the midst of
the most terrifying experience of my life, lying there
frozen on the ground from some alien technology, I was able
to look up at him and somehow sense that what he was
saying was true -- he wasn't there to hurt me.

He tapped two buttons on his watch.

"Okay, you're unfrozen again. Now, I'm trusting you, and for the last time, you have to trust us. We are not the only aliens on Earth at the moment. We've gotta get off of the plan—"

He didn't get a chance to finish his sentence, because just then, a turquoise blue laser beam zapped the ground beside us, scorching the earth. My heart skipped five beats as I jumped up. Ari went wide-eyed and grabbed my arm.

"Come on!" he shouted, pulling me toward the ship.

I glanced back over my shoulder and saw them — two large, black spaceships swooping through the sky, like Pterodactyls, swaying back and forth in the strangest of patterns. They came soaring down over our farm, firing a flurry of laser beams from their wings. Ari and I sprinted back toward the ship in a criss-cross pattern, running for our lives. As we reached the orb, Celeste leaned down and yanked us right inside.

"Oh, sure, now you want to come with us," she said.

She slammed the door and we all scrambled back to our seats. I latched the safety harness around my waist as Celeste hit a series of switches.

"Okay, kid, try not to puke up all that birthday cake."

I stared at her, incredulous, as she slammed the gearstick and we went rolling across the field. Above us, the attacking ships were weaving around the sky in strange patterns, firing laser beams down at the ground.

"Celeste, if you get us out of this, I'll give you my allowance for the next three months," said Ari.

"I'm gonna hold you to that, bro," she grinned.

I clutched the armrests of my seat and stared out the front windshield. As we picked up speed, the giant sphere went rolling around the fields, crushing stalks of corn, cutting left and right. Amazingly, within the ship we didn't spin or rotate. Like some kind of gyroscope, we were staying perfectly balanced on the inside. I watched in awe as Celeste skillfully avoided the oncoming maelstrom, dodging in and out of the laser beams that fell like rain.

"Preparing for liftoff," she said, as we soared into the sky.

"Lookout," shouted Ari. "Three O'clock!"

"I see them," replied Celeste, slamming the controls.

I nearly did puke up Katie's birthday cake just then, but I managed to hold it in, more fascinated than I was airsick. To my amazement, Celeste suddenly steered the ship right into the flurry of laser beams, flying directly for the attacking ships.

"What are you doing? You're headed right into them!" shouted Ari.

"Which one of us here graduated from flight school?"

"You did," he answered, shutting up.

She pushed harder on the controls and we hit maximum speed, cutting a path right between the oncoming starfighters! I held my breath as we squeezed between them, climbing higher and higher into the sky. By the time they realized what had happened, we were long gone.

As we made for the clouds, I turned around and looked out the rear window of the UFO. There, I saw my house receding into the distance. It would be the last time I'd see it for a couple of days. As I watched it longingly, I spotted the small figure of my grandfather running out onto the porch with his shotgun, staring in awe at the strange geometrical tracks that had been left in our fields.

Chapter 3.   ARI & CELESTE

The next thing I knew, Mars was going by in the window. I don't know how we got there so fast, I mean, to me, inside the ship, it felt like we were going 65 m.p.h. on a Kansas City Highway.   But within 10 minutes of leaving Earth, there it was, the awesome-looking Red Planet, suspended out in space, filling my entire view. As we went whipping around it in an elliptical path, I could see red dust sweeping over the bumpy terrain.

Ari and Celeste hadn't said a word since we left Earth. They were still too occupied with setting coordinates and reading spacemaps, which were unfolded all over Ari's lap. But at the sight of Mars, they both relaxed a little.

"I think we're probably safe now," said Celeste.

She set the ship on auto-pilot and rotated her Captain's chair around, facing me.

"So? Pretty cool, huh?" she said.

I didn't say anything.

"Alan? You there?" she asked, snapping her fingers.

"How do you know my name?" I asked.

"Oh, we know lots about you," said Ari, coming back and sitting beside me. "I don't know how to tell you this, bro, but we've been listening to your radio show for the last 8 months."

I was stunned. They what?! I mean, I always suspected someone might be listening, but since I never got any responses, I figured I was pretty much talking to myself. Over time, I'd grown more and more comfortable with my broadcasts, constantly talking about my personal life. Anyone who listened to every episode would certainly know a great deal about me. In my head, I went racing back through the transmissions, wondering if I'd said anything too embarrassing. Suddenly, "The Alan Albright Show" didn't seem like such a great idea anymore.

"You're a funny, dude," said Ari. "You keep us entertained for hours."

"And because we're so interested in you, we decided to break a few rules and come get you," said Celeste.

"Not an easy thing to do, by the way, abducting an Earthling," said Ari. "I found a secret way into your planet's atmosphere, over Antarctica."

"Yeah, real secret. The E.P.A. found us, Ari!" said Celeste.

"But not 'til the last minute. I bought us a lot of time.

Come on, give it up, sis, you know I rocked today—"

"Your ego is bigger than Uranus, I swear," said Celeste, rolling her eyes.

"What's the E.P.A.?" I asked, utterly confused.

"The Earthling Protection Agency. They were the ones who attacked us," said Ari.

"The Earthling Protection Agency?" I said. "But they almost killed me!"

"Those were freeze-rays they were using. They were trying to capture us," said Ari.

"Their job is to make sure Earthlings don't get into outer space, no matter what. Ninety percent of the time it works out in your guys' favor. But occasionally things get out of control," said Celeste. "Like today."

"Which is why this is such a big deal," said Ari, putting his feet up on the dashboard. "Alan, when you get back to Earth, tell all your friends you were abducted by an amazingly cool kid from outer space named Ari Centauri."

Celeste rolled her eyes.

"Ari's just dying for someone on Earth to write a book about him."

"That's ridiculous," said Ari. "The reason I want

Alan to tell everyone he was abducted is because the more stories that are told about aliens, the better. That's the whole point, Celeste, and you know it. It keeps the myth alive."

"What myth?" I said.

"You know, whether or not there's such a thing as extraterrestrial life," said Ari. "Which as you can see, there is. But we don't want you Earthlings to know yet. So the more stories that are told about aliens, the more they're going to contradict each other, the more you Earthlings don't know what's going on. It's a smoke screen."

"Why can't we know about aliens?" I said.

"Frankly? Because you're uncivilized," said Ari. "At least that's what the League of Planets has ruled."

"Uncivilized--?" I said.

"Well, yeah," said Ari. "For example, do you know that Earthlings are the only species in the entire known universe who actually destroy their own planet? No one else does that. Not even the Aborgisians are that dumb. But you guys, you're ruining your own environment, and you know it, and yet you keep doing it. It's idiotic."

I suddenly went quiet, feeling a little awkward. I didn't have any response.

"Sorry, Alan. But there won't be any big intergalactic introduction until Earth evolves. And right now, you're going the other way. You're devolving. Who knows how Earthlings would respond if aliens just showed up one day?"

I was a little offended. I mean, yes, on the one hand, if a bunch of UFOs came flying out of the skies back home, it might trigger World War 3. But on the other hand, I didn't like the way Ari kept putting down Earth. I was starting to feel a strange, new feeling: Planetary pride.

"Where are you guys from?" I said.

"Alpha Centauri, about 4 light-years away. I'm Celeste and this meteorhead here is my brother Ari."

"Are you guys human?"

They both started laughing.

"Of course. What do we look like, Horolgulums?"

I did a double-take, confused.

"Technically speaking, we're from Earth, just like you. Or at least, our ancestors were," said Celeste.

"How's that possible?" I said.

"10,000 years ago, most people on Earth lived in the city of Atlantis," said Ari. "You ever heard of Atlantis?"

"Of course," I said, curious where this was going. "I thought it was made up."

"Uh-uh," said Ari. "Atlantis was real. Unfortunately, it got hit by a giant Flood, and so all the citizens had to evacuate. They were brilliant people, way smarter than people on Earth now — like I said, you're devolving — and so they built spaceships and went off into outer space and settled on other planets. And that's how human beings got into space."

'Amazing,' I thought. Was this really our true history?

"How come no one on Earth knows this?" I said.

"The Flood destroyed everything. There's probably lots of artifacts and clues buried in Earth's oceans, but no one will ever find them. Atlantis will stay a myth, just like extraterrestrials."

"How many other planets have humans on them?" I said.

"Oh, man, I don't know. What do you think Celeste?"

"Hundreds," she said. "The original seven colonies from Atlantis spawned more colonies which spawned more colonies, until societies were set up on planets in almost every galaxy. There's a lot going on up here, Alan. Once you Earthlings build better ships, you'll discover it all."

As I tried to process everything she was saying, Celeste launched into detailed descriptions of our surroundings, like a cosmic tour guide.

"Outside the starboard window you can see Phobos and Deimos, the two moons of Mars. And straight ahead is the asteroid belt. Don't worry, it didn't give me any trouble on the way in."

Sure enough, as I looked out the front windshield, I saw thousands of giant boulders tumbling slowly through space. Celeste managed to navigate them beautifully and before I knew it we emerged safely on the other side, zooming past Saturn, Uranus and Neptune. By the time we reached Pluto, I couldn't get the stupid grin off of my face.

Celeste even let me fly the ship for a few minutes, giving me a few pointers, showing me how to use the Y-shaped steering wheel and how to swoop up and down using a long lever imbedded in the dashboard called "the plunger". It was an amazing ride, but after ten minutes, Celeste took control of the ship back from me.

"That was the scenic part, Alan. I took it slow so you could see everything. But now we're going into deep space. Sorta like going from the country roads onto the highway, if you know what I mean. I'm going to increase our speed exponentially. You'll need to strap in."

I must have looked a little nervous because Ari came back and helped me out, locking me into another safety harness. This one came down over my head, like a foam-padded bar on a roller coaster.

"This can be pretty rough," said Ari. "Roughest part of the trip. Here's the vomit vacuum if you need it."

He handed me a long, flexible tube extending from the wall of the ship.

"Alright Alan, let's see what you Earthlings are made of," shouted Celeste.

She pushed forward on the "plunger" in the center of the control panel and immediately the ship pitched forward, diving straight down. It felt like we were on a speeding train with no tracks in sight. And we weren't slowing down either. We just kept plummeting and plummeting downward, until I swear I felt my belly roll up into my chest. I held the vomit vacuum up to my mouth as I focused all my attention on my stomach muscles. I held on with everything I had. The ship rattled violently as we went further and deeper into space. The light grew darker inside the hull and there were fewer and fewer stars to be seen outside the window.

Finally, just at the point when I thought I couldn't hold it in any longer, we came to a stop. It sent me forward out of my seat a few inches knocking the wind out of my gut. I gasped, and the ship resumed a gentle, cruising speed. Everything seemed back to normal. I looked over to find Ari staring at me.

"Heck of a ride, huh?" he said.

I nodded. Up front, Celeste flicked a switch on the ceiling.

"Gentlemen," she said, "We are now making our final approach to the Alpha Centauri System, where the local time is 3:00pm – If you'd kindly stay seated, I'll have you on the ground shortly."

"You are such a dork," Ari said to her.

"A dork who got us back and forth from Earth without getting blown to pieces. I'd say you owe me big-time, brother."

Suddenly, the UFO tilted forward again, and right out the front windshield I saw the surface of their home planet come into view. It was absolutely beautiful, a giant ball of blue and green that resembled Earth in many ways, except it had more water. The only landmass was just a large dot in the center of the ocean.

"That's our planet, New Atlantis," said Ari.

The pitch-blackness of space gave way to a beautiful blue sky as we entered the planet's atmosphere, which was filled with white and pink clouds. That's when I first realized there were two suns lighting up the sky. Celeste saw me staring in at them, and elaborated.

"We're a binary star system. We have two suns, Alpha Centauri A, and Alpha Centauri B, which means we get a lot more daylight than Earth."

"Which brings us to something else," said Ari, turning to me. "Your eyes."

"What about them? I said.

"Everyone on our planet has brown eyes—"

"Some have black," corrected Celeste.

"Okay, yes some have black, and some have brown, and some have charcoal and some have whatever," he said, twirling his fingers. "The point is they're all dark. It's because we have so much sunlight — light colored eyes got weeded out of our genes. But you, Alan, well..."

I was starting to see where he was going with this.

"You're going to stand out. I mean, your eyes are very

pretty, don't get me wrong," he said, teasing me. "But they're blue. Anyone who takes a good look at you is going to know you're from Earth. And we don't want them to know that. Yet."

"Okay," I said. "So what do we do?"

"Wear these," he said.

He removed a pair of dark wraparound sunglasses from his pocket. They were sort of cool, all black.

"Try them on."

I did. Everything became tinted.

"You look good — like a vegan," said Ari.

I turned my head from side to side, taking in the view as we came gliding down over a busy cityscape. There were vast, sprawling buildings lining cobblestone streets and odd structures that had curved walls and domed roofs, which made it feel old-fashioned. But there were also neon billboards and glowing signs, advertising everything from intergalactic restaurants to 4D movies, which made it feel futuristic.

The hovercraft spaceship traffic was intense. Somehow, thousands of flying vehicles were managing to move through the city at extremely fast speeds without crashing into each other. There were at least 10 levels to the traffic, from low-level, just above the street, to all the way up over our heads, past the clouds. In fact, when we first approached the city, I thought those were buildings I was looking at, only to realize as we drew closer that they were pillars of flying cars.

Celeste had been a brilliant pilot so far, but as we approached the main intersection of town, a towering, criss-crossing network of ships, I got nervous. She jammed the joystick forward and we went swooping upward into a flowing column of spaceships. Then, just at the right moment, she pulled the stick left and we entered a horizontal row of them, keeping up with the traffic. She was doing great and I was just about ready to trust her, when suddenly, she dove toward street level again and I accidentally let out a very wimpy scream.

"Stop showing off," said Ari. "You're scaring him."

"Don't worry, Alan. I've never been in a crash."

"You've had your license for 6 months!" said Ari.

"And I've never crashed," she said.

I turned my attention out the window to keep my mind off the possibility of a collision. Hundreds of small little shops went by in a blur, hawking everything from colorful arts and crafts to the newest technological wonders. The

People of New Atlantis were out and about, bustling in the streets. I noticed their clothes. Most of the men wore robes, like the style of dress you might find in ancient Rome. They were a little bit boring. But the women were clad extravagantly in multi-colored fashions, the kind of stuff you see on the runway at a Paris fashion show, but you don't think anyone actually ever wears. Well, the women were wearing it here, and wearing it well.

"Check it out, Alan," said Celeste, "Right around this turn is the main part of the city. Andromeda Square, named after one of our greatest politicians, Andromeda Aldebaran."

She whipped us around a turn and we emerged into an intersection of streets, all mish-mashing into each other, meeting in a large, fenced-in grassy area. This was the only place I'd seen up until now where there were actually some tall buildings. In the center of it all was a domed structure that reminded me of pictures I'd seen of the Sydney Opera House, or the Justice League of America building where Superman and his friends lived. It was arched, resembling a gigantic "A", and there were long, wide steps leading up to it.

"That's Government Hall," said Celeste.

"Our dad works there," added Ari. "He's a pretty important Senator."

"Yeah, that's another reason we can't get caught with you," said Celeste. "Not only would we get in trouble, but it would look really, really bad for our father if anyone found out we were involved in an Earthling abduction."

"Well, it's not gonna get out, is it?" said Ari, turning to me. "Now, let's go over the plan. We're taking you to a party. And not just any party — the biggest party of the year, thrown by Teddy Zee, the craziest kid in our school. You're gonna meet kids from all over the place, maybe even some non-humans."

"Non-humans?" I said.

"Yeah — Horseheads, Serpentines, Horologiums — Teddy's a popular kid. His parties are pretty much known throughout the galaxies. So you'll probably see these strange looking dudes hanging around. You just have to play it cool, like it's nothing new to you."

"I can do that."

"Oh man, kids are gonna flip when we introduce you."

I wondered what he meant by 'introduce me', but

didn't think too long about it, as Celeste steered the ship down a side street. We glided through a suburban area, until finally, I spotted a house ahead in the distance. I knew right away it was "Teddy Zee's" house. How did I know? Because it was a zoo. There were hovercrafts and spaceships parked all over the lawn and also up and down the street. There were teenagers standing around in groups on the grass, while others formed a line just to get in the front door. Loud, strange music was coming from inside and there were people dancing everywhere.

"You okay, Alan?" said Celeste.

I went silent, realizing that to everyone at this party, I was the alien.

Chapter 4. TEDDY ZEE'S INTERGALACTIC JAMMER

Celeste landed gently on the grass and parked among the other ships. As we climbed down the metal staircase, I was immediately engulfed by hundreds of kids on the front lawn who were sipping colorful drinks through curly-Q straws attached to strange glass containers. A few of them looked me over as we strode across the grass, but I just kept moving. Behind the tinted sunglasses, my eyes were darting around the scene, fascinated.

Suddenly, I caught sight of my first non-human alien, just across the lawn, chatting to some of his friends. I didn't know it at the time, but he was a Lyrian, an Insectoid with Grasshopper features, and he was so shocking-looking that from the first moment I saw him, I couldn't stop staring. His midsection was a shiny greenish-brown color and scaly and his arms had little jagged spikes running down the length of them. He was leaning against the side of the house, talking to a girl who looked human. What was amazing to me was how casual they both looked. Clearly, kids in space were used to hanging out with alien races that looked completely different from them, but since it was new to me, I have to admit, I was a little freaked out. I just couldn't stop staring.

Suddenly, the Lyrian's long, skinny antennae twitched and he glanced over at me. It was like he could sense me gawking, and he didn't like it one bit. The next thing I knew, he squatted down on powerful legs and leapt through the air, arcing over the crowd, landing right in front of me. It happened so fast I had no time to react.

"You got a problem?" he said, jamming a finger in my chest.

I think I managed to stutter 'no' when Ari suddenly appeared.

"Whoa, Stanley, easy, man. This is my friend, Alan. It's his first time at one of Teddy Zee's parties. He's just a little bit overwhelmed."

"Why's he staring at me?" said Stanley.

"Well who wouldn't? You're the best looking Insectoid in the Lyrian system, Stanley. I mean, you turn heads when you go out."

Ari put an arm around me, grinning.

"Tell him you're sorry, man."

"Sorry, man," I said.

Stanley thought about it.

"I'll cut him a break, 'cause he's your friend, Centauri. But if I catch you staring at me again -- "

I shook my head, assuring him that wouldn't be a problem. He finally squatted back down, bent his legs, and sprung up into the sky, disappearing into the crowd.

"I told you not to stare," whispered Ari.

"I couldn't help it," I said.

"Those Lyrians have tempers," said Ari. "They're generally nice enough, but they're a little insecure about the way they look."

He continued leading me through the crowd, past some extremely cool spaceships parked haphazardly across the grass. As we passed the cockpit of one, I saw a couple kissing inside, but the guy reached out and tapped the glass window and it tinted black. We continued toward the front door, where Ari cut the line and slipped right inside. People either knew who he was or just didn't want to start a fight, because they didn't say anything as we entered.

Walking into Teddy's House was like walking into a dream within a dream. I had already been in a state of semi-shock from my trip through outer space. But in there, I experienced true sensory onslaught. I didn't know where to look first: at the dance floor, where a hundred teenagers of all different species were dancing with feverish frenzy; or toward the holographic television set in the middle of the room, a circular, pie-shaped table that generated a colorful 3-D image with no box around it. Groups of kids were huddled everywhere and the strange, alien music was pounding out with a rapid-fire beat. I didn't know how anyone could dance to it, but they were. I saw a couple of girls zooming around the house on rocket-propelled rollerskates, giggling and chasing each other through the crowd. And in the corner there was a group of guys dancing in mid-air, doing acrobatic break-dancing moves. They were all wearing glowing boots, which I could only presume were anti-gravity boots. Suddenly, someone bumped into me.

"May I interest you in an appetizer?" came a monotone voice.

I looked to see a child-size black and white robot on wheels, carrying a serving tray. I studied the food, figured it looked good enough and tasted it. It was a creamy pastry, like an éclair.

"Spacey-Cakes," said Ari, grabbing one for himself, stuffing the whole thing in his mouth at once. He took another, wiping the platter clean.

"Mmmm. Out of this world," he said, singing, making a little air-guitar with his hands. Then he looked at me.

"Oh, I forgot, you don't know that commercial."

"No," I said, chewing.

Celeste appeared, squeezing between two burly guys.

"Ugh, when can we get out of here? I'm starting to get claustrophobic."

"As soon as I do what I came to do," said Ari. "Hey, I think I see Teddy Zee."

He navigated a path through the crowd until finally we reached the other side of the room. There, a 14 year old boy in a silver blazer with a flashing tie and white pants was holding court, telling stories to his friends, who were all laughing. A couple of them weren't completely human, including a very feline looking humanoid girl, with wide-set cat eyes, pointed ears and a cute button nose. I actually would have found her pretty if it weren't for the whiskers.

Suddenly, the kid in the silver blazer looked up and saw Ari.

"Centauri! I was wondering if you were gonna show."

"Are you kidding, Teddy?" Ari shot back. "I told you, I'm gonna blast the roof off this place. I'm gonna make this the most memorable party of the year."

"I hope so, man, I hope so," said Teddy, turning to me. "Who's your friend in the shades?"

"Teddy, I'd like you to meet Alan."

Teddy looked me up and down.

"How you doing?"

I just nodded and smiled.

"He's not from around here," said Ari.

"No duh," said Teddy, laughing. "So what system are you from?"

I stood there, silent, like an idiot.

"Vega," said Ari.

"Vega?! They certainly know how to party out in Vega. And you came all the way here? You must have heard Teddy Zee throws the best jammers in the galaxy," said Teddy.

"So when are we doing this contest, Teddy?" Ari said.

"Just waitin' on you, bro," said Teddy, grinning.

He suddenly jumped over the couch and lowered the volume on his stereo, fading the music out. The party came to an abrupt stop as everyone turned in his direction. Teddy hopped up onto the Holographic Television stand, breaking up the image.

"Ladies and Gentlemen, Aliens of all Planets, allow me to welcome you to this festive occasion, as we celebrate the end of school and the beginning of summer!"

Everybody cheered.

"Now," continued Teddy. "As you all know, my family is dirty, filthy, stinking rich. My parents recently bought me a brand new Meteorite X-15 hovercraft, rendering my old, piece of junk Asteroid 3i pretty much useless. So I've decided to give it away. It's my annual 'show and tell' competition. Whoever brought the coolest thing to my party, from any part of the universe, wins my ship. So who's up?"

Suddenly, a boy named Johnny Crater stepped forward.

"I'll go," he said.

"Johnny Crater. The fastest kid in the Freshman class, track star supreme. What do you got for me, Johnny?

Johnny held up a cage that looked like a tackle box.

"Alright everyone, you might want to stand back. This creature can be a little feisty," he said.

"What is it?" shouted a nervous girl in the back, as Johnny began to open the cage door.

"It's an Aborgesian Toad, all the way from Eridanus. I flew down there yesterday, chased it all through the marsh. I caught it with my own two hands."

Suddenly, the metal door crashed open by itself, and Johnny dropped the containment unit. The Aborgesian Toad came bouncing out of the box, right into the middle of the room. The thing looked like a frog, but it was much larger, the size of a pot-bellied pig. It had squat, thin legs and was seated back on its haunches, glancing around at us with round eyes. I noticed it also had two razor-sharp vampire fangs coming down over its lips.

Suddenly, it looked right in my direction, opened its mouth, and fired its tongue like a bullwhip. It unfurled across the room, hurtling right towards me! At the very last second I dodged out of the way and the tongue went swooshing over my shoulder, smacking the wall behind me. It hit with a splat and stuck there for a second like Silly Putty. All the kids stared at the enormous Toad with its tongue stretched across the room and started laughing. Then, without missing a beat, Johnny Crater dove across the floor and caught the creature in between his hands. The Aborgesian Toad croaked and retracted its tongue, as Johnny squeezed the thing back into its cage and quickly slammed the door. All the kids applauded.

"Good show, good show," said Teddy Zee, impressed. "That's gonna be a tough act to follow. Okay, who's next?"

Rigil Kentaurus stepped forward, a very smart-looking kid wearing a brown space suit and thin, metallic glasses. He cleared his throat and addressed the crowd.

"I ventured on this endeavor mainly for academic reasons. I delighted in the challenge of finding the most unique biological specimen in our galaxy, and I think I've succeeded. My friends, I present to you, Acid Worms, from the Chameleon system."

Like a magician, Rigil reached into his vest pocket and whipped out a plastic bag filled with powdery, red dirt. There were three long, reddish-green worms slithering around inside. The circle of kids closed in for a better look.

"This is a uranium-lined bag so they can't eat through it. However, Teddy, if you wouldn't mind, might I use your coffee table?"

"Go ahead," said Teddy.

"They'll probably ruin it," cautioned Rigil.

"Don't worry. I'll buy a new one before my parents get back."

Rigil walked over to the coffee table in the center of Teddy's living room, took the bag of dirt and dumped it out all over. The slimy looking worms crawled out and inched their way across the piece of furniture. Suddenly, there was a hissing sound, and smoke began to rise, as one of the Acid Worms sizzled straight down through the top of the table. A moment later, the other two did the same. I watched amazed as they dropped down through their respective holes and landed on the floor. All the kids gasped and backed up.

"Stand back, they'll eat right through your toes," said Rigil.

He laid the bag open on the floor, right in front of the worms, and they crawled back in.

"I excavated these all by myself, I'll have you know."

There was a smattering of applause as Teddy Zee stepped forward again, sort of rolling his eyes to the crowd.

"Well, I don't know if that beats the Aborgesian Toad, but cool. Good job, Rigil. Alright, who's next? You ready Centauri?

"Is it my turn?" said Ari, grinning.

"Come on, don't keep me in suspense any longer. You said you were gonna blow the roof off this place. What've you got?"

Ari waited a moment for dramatic effect.

"Well, unlike Rigil, I didn't partake in this competition for 'academic reasons'."

He made quotes with his fingers and everyone laughed except Rigil.

"No, me, I want the ship. Our family needs a second one, because Celeste here is way too good a pilot, and she always winds up flying everywhere. And I'm sick of it. I want my own ride."

Everyone laughed.

"Okay, so?" said Teddy Zee, dying.

"So, I'm in it to win it. And if I was going to win this thing, I knew I had to bring something nobody else would bring. Something nobody else would dare have the courage to go and get. Something only Ari Centauri could pull off."

"For the love of God, Centauri, what is it?" said Teddy.

"An Earthling."

The room went quiet. I was stunned. I turned bright red, even though nobody was even looking at me. I heard the scattered sounds of laughter and muttering. Teddy Zee starting cracking up.

"Yeah, right. Good one, Centauri. I knew you were

full of it. Alright, come on, who really has something to show off?"

"I'm not joking, Teddy," said Ari. "Celeste and I went to Earth and brought a kid back with us. A human boy. And he's here right now."

Whispers started to trickle through the room. The teenagers all looked around, curious. Finally, Ari grinned and pointed a finger straight in my direction.

"Everyone, meet Alan," he said.

In one instant, I felt the eyes of the party sweep towards me.

"Take off your sunglasses, Al. Show'em."

'Show'em?!' I thought, embarrassed. I can specifically remember my point of view at that moment, peering out through those tinted shades, wishing with all my heart that I didn't have to lower them. While in some ways it was cool to be the center of attention, I couldn't stop this nagging feeling in the back of my mind that this was all going to lead to trouble. Finally, knowing I didn't really have a choice, I lowered my sunglasses.

I guess my blue eyes were enough to pass the test, because there was a collective gasp from the crowd. One girl nearly fainted, stumbling back into her group of friends who luckily caught her. Teddy Zee threw his arms up in the air and spun around, like he couldn't take what he was seeing. As far as me, I just stood there, really unsure as to what the proper thing to do would be. Finally I just raised my hand and waved.

"Hey," I said.

A few boys muttered stunned expressions behind me, and even backed off, like I was radioactive or something. I turned my head one way, and that side of the room backed up. Then I turned it the other way, and the other side did the same thing. Ari was directly ahead of me, chuckling, enjoying every moment of it. He stepped forward and put an arm around me.

"You don't have to be afraid of him. He's cool."

Teddy Zee cautiously stepped up.

"Are you really from Earth, kid?"

"Kansas City, Missouri. United States. Earth. Yeah," I said.

"Look at those peepers," said Teddy Zee, leaning in real close to me. "Very cool."

Rigil Kentaurus was the next kid "brave" enough to come check me out. He strode up, about a foot taller than me, studying me like a scientist.

"Fascinating," he said.

"He's not a specimen," said Celeste. "He's just like us."

"Well, not exactly," Rigil said, correcting him. "There's a 1 percent genetic difference between Earthlings and Alpha Centaurians."

The rest of the kids came over, closing in on me. Teddy Zee seemed blown away.

"You guys really went down to Earth and abducted him yourselves? Are you crazy? That's illegal!"

"I told him it was moronic," said Celeste, pointing at Ari. "But he doesn't listen. He said he was going with or without me, and without me, he would've gotten himself killed."

"You're a braver man than I am," said Teddy Zee to Ari. "What if your dad finds out?"

"Well he's not gonna find out, is he, Teddy?" said Ari, loud enough so that he was really addressing the entire room. "My parents are gone until tomorrow morning. And we're taking Alan back to Earth tonight."

A short girl approached me, curious.

"Have you been to New York City?" she said.

"Once," I said.

"What about Disneyland?" said a voice from the crowd.

"Yeah," I said.

"Did you go on Space Mountain?"

"Lots of times," I said.

The crowd seemed seriously impressed by this and started to move in closer.

"Can I touch you?" said a strange non-human girl, reaching out a skinny purple finger. I think she was female but I can't be positive. I wasn't sure whether to say yes or not.

"Alright," said Celeste, pushing her away, "That's enough."

Teddy Zee nodded in agreement, putting his arm around me.

"Celeste is right, give the kid a break. He's only got one day in outer space and I don't think he wants to spend it answering a bunch of stupid questions."

He turned to Ari.

"Look, the contest is officially over. Clearly Ari and Celeste are the winners. Congratulations, you guys get my ship," he reached into his pocket and tossed them the keys.

"Enjoy her. I don't know how much life she's got left."

Ari caught the keys and raised his hands to the crowd, to scattered applause. Teddy squeezed me tighter.

"As for Alan here, what do you say we show him how we party in outer space?" he said, shouting.

The entire crowd cheered and started chanting my name, which was weird. Teddy jumped across the room, flicked the stereo on, and the party kicked back into high gear. Before I knew what was happening, I was surrounded by a dance floor of bouncing kids, facing an Alpha Centaurian girl who was looking at me with big brown eyes. She was jumping all around, swinging her head, flicking her long ponytail like a helicopter. I smiled and tried to keep up with her, but I'm not a good dancer. She grabbed my hands and started moving my arms back and forth in some strange alien version of The Twist.

"My name's Jupiter," she said.

"I'm Alan," I said.

"So? What do you think of the Alpha Centauri system?" she asked.

"It's far out," I said, and she laughed. She twirled us both around, much to my surprise.

"I've always wanted to go to Earth," she said. "My

older brother did it once with his friends, when he turned 18, you know, on a dare. I think it would be fun."

"It's a great planet," I said.

"Do you think if I visited, I could stay with you, Alan?"

"Sure," I shrugged.

"Don't worry," she suddenly added, "I'd probably never have the guts to make the trip anyway. It's like 4 light-years away. I can't believe Celeste Centauri actually did it. She's a pretty amazing girl, you know."

I stared across the room at Celeste, who was standing against the wall with her arms folded. Finally the song came to an end and I stopped moving, exhausted. Jupiter and I stared at each other for a moment, breathing hard, and then suddenly...

She kissed me. I barely had time to react before she leaned in and planted one right on my mouth.

"Sorry," she said. "I've just always wanted to kiss an Earthling."

Suddenly a deafening, piercing siren blared out. Everyone froze and looked toward the windows. Several spaceships were descending through the air with flashing lights, landing right on Teddy Zee's front lawn. The entire party realized what was happening at once. Someone screamed "cops", and then all the teenagers scattered like cockroaches, heading for the exits. Kids started climbing out windows, and in the mad rush, I was instantly spun around and separated from Jupiter. In fact, I didn't know where I was, or where any of the doors were. Kids went whipping by me in all directions. I suddenly started to feel extremely anxious and panicked. I began hyperventilating, a condition which I still haven't altogether cured myself of when things get tense. I thought I was about to faint. As I stood there wheezing, I suddenly felt a hand on my arm. I looked up to see Ari.

"Back entrance. Celeste's meeting us there."

I didn't need to move my feet, because Ari practically dragged me away, barging through the crowd. He pulled me down a back hallway which not many people seemed to know about, into the rear of the enormous house. We reached the end of a corridor and he pushed a button on the wall. A door I didn't even realize was there opened up and we hurried outside, into the backyard.

Celeste was already driving the spherical ship across the grass, spinning towards us. She pulled the orb up and pushed open the door as we climbed in, frantic.

"What about your new ship?" she said.

"I'll pick it up tomorrow, just go, go, go!" Ari screamed at her, scrambling up the ladder. Celeste didn't hesitate, yanking the accelerator and sending us flying off across the front lawn. She pulled back on the plunger and we started to ascend, lifting off the ground, soaring into the sky. I turned and peered out the back window to see crowds of kids fleeing Teddy Zee's space party, scattering off in all directions.

Chapter 5.   THE AKASHIC RECORDS

"I can't believe you told everyone like that, Ari! Honestly, sometimes I think you've got a black hole in your head," shouted Celeste as she piloted us across space.

"I'm sorry, I'm sorry... I wanted to present Alan to our friend's with some dramatic flair. You know me, sis. I'm a showboat," he said, turning to me. "You're not mad at me, are you bro?"

"You could have told me beforehand," I said.

"Oh, please, you had a great time. I saw you 'dancing' with Jupiter Jones," he said, and I had to laugh.

"Whatever, you blew our cover," said Celeste, still angry. "For all we know, the police were there for us. Somebody probably turned us in."

"Okay, now you're being paranoid..."

"No, I'm not. It's too dangerous, Ari. You ruined everything. I want to take Alan back to Earth."

"Oh, come on, we ditched them! Look," he said and pointed to the dashboard. "The radar's clear for half a parsec. No ships anywhere. Nobody's following us."

"Unless they're cloaked," she said.

Ari rolled his eyes.

"Look, we're safe, and I wanna take Alan to the Akashic Records. Heck, it was your idea to go in the first place!"

"What's the Akashic Records?" I said, interrupting.

"Only like the most amazing museum in the entire universe," said Ari. "Celeste and I agreed that we'd each get to show you one thing special in outer space. I wanted to take you to Teddy Zee's party, and she wanted to take you to an intergalactic history museum. Says a lot about her character, doesn't it? Now come on Celeste, we didn't bring him half way across the universe just to turn around and take him right back home again."

*   *   *   *   *

Celeste finally gave in and twenty minutes later we arrived at the Akashic Records, located on a pretty, purple planet in the constellation Corona Borealis. There was lot of approaching traffic, thousands of visitors coming from all parts of the world to view the universe's number one tourist attraction.

We landed in the parking lot of the grand plaza,

where eight government-looking buildings formed an octagonal plaza, each with enormous columns and triangular, pitched roofs. The Main Building had a marble staircase leading to the wide-mouthed opening and there were long lines of people gathered on the steps, waiting to get in.

"I say we do the group tour," said Celeste.

"Aw, come on, that's so boring," said Ari.

"I want Alan to actually learn things about space while he's here. And you learn more with a guide."

Celeste wasn't budging and personally I didn't care either way — I was just excited to get inside. Finally Ari relented and we joined a group of families waiting on the museum's front steps. Our tour guide, like everyone else's tour guide, was a holographic projection wearing a vest and bowtie. It was weird, because even though he wasn't real, I could feel his friendliness coming through.

"Hello," he said, as we followed him through the main doors, "Welcome to the Akashic Records. My name is Bootes and I will be your Hologuide for the next sixty minutes. If you have any questions, please feel free to ask. I am a completely interactive form of artificial intelligence."

I looked around and suddenly realized we were standing in a massive, marble corridor, the length of a football field. Running along both sides of the hallway were dozens of gargantuan statues, depicting famous characters and figures from across the galaxies.

"You are currently in the Hall of Heroes," said Bootes. "This corridor stands in tribute to heroic individuals whose actions or ideas have helped make the universe a better place."

The first sculpture we passed was a giant humanoid, a cross between a man and a rhinoceros. It was nearly 3 stories tall, with a long, leathery torso and a big horn on its head. The face was fierce and powerful, with sharp, black eyes.

"This is Monoceros. One of the greatest warriors the universe has ever known. 5,000 years ago, he led his planet out of slavery and helped them earn a seat in the League of Planets. A real hero."

Some of the parents took pictures, using cool cameras that produced instant 3D holograms that you could hold in your hand. As we moved on to the next statue, we saw a very dignified looking man, with spectacles resting on the tip of his nose. He carried a thick text under his armpit, and kept his other hand tucked into the vest pocket of his suit.

"Dr. Aquarius Farholm," said Bootes. "Esteemed humanitarian and animal rights activist. He single-handedly rescued the marine life of Pisces Austrinus by rerouting fresh water into that sector when their natural resources became polluted. He saved over 100 planets in his lifetime and is recognized as a hero throughout the universe."

A few people whispered to each other, impressed with Dr. Aquarius Farholm's accomplishments. Celeste leaned over to me.

"He's one of my heroes. I want to work for his foundation someday."

"Doing what?" I said.

"Helping impoverished star systems in other galaxies. There are so many people that need our help."

The group moved along to the next statue. It was a beautiful human woman.

"And this is someone you all probably know, someone I truly admired," said the hologram. "Andromeda Aldebaran."

She looked like an elegant woman, somebody whose eyes had seen a lot. In fact, she looked kind of familiar. It was hard to tell, because she wore a glittering crown and had long, flowing hair, but, well, there's no other way to say it — she looked exactly like my mother!

I was astonished. I mean, the hair was different, long when my mom's was short, but the other facial features were similar enough that I went silent and just stared at the sculpture for a minute. Her body was carved out of smooth marble, and she was standing in a relaxed pose, hands by her side, chin tilted to the heavens, graceful.

"What's wrong?" whispered Celeste, noticing my reaction. I didn't say anything for a long time. Then I raised my hand.

"Excuse me, who was she exactly?" I said.

The Hologuide seemed delighted to have a question.

"Andromeda Aldebaran was a brilliant politician who negotiated the well known Syrian-Gray treaty. Not so long ago, those two races were intent on destroying each other. It was a dangerous war for all the neighboring galaxies, with enough nuclear force to wipe out entire planets. But somehow, using the gentle persuasion that was hers and hers alone, Andromeda Aldebaran convinced the leaders of each race to call a truce. The Syrian-Gray treaty was signed over a decade ago and has held up to this day. Of course, she is best known for having originally come from Earth, the only Earthling _ever_ to participate in Intergalactic Politics."

"Is she still alive?" I said.

"Nobody knows for sure," said Bootes. "Just after the Syrian-Gray treaty was signed, Andromeda Aldebaran and her husband, Atlas Aldebaran, announced their retirement. They disappeared from public life and nobody has seen them since. Theories abound that they were eventually caught and killed by their enemies, but I for one find it rather grim to presume they're dead."

I took one last lingering look at the statue as our tour finally moved away.

*   *   *   *   *

Our last stop in the Akashic Records was the world-famous holographic theater, which immerses you directly into a historical scene. The presentation we were shown was called *Dinosaurs, Where Are They Now?* and I remember immediately thinking, 'Dinosaurs — Where Are They Now? I'll tell you where they are. They're extinct!' Everybody knew that, right?

Suddenly, booming music came out of a powerful sound system, and a giant holographic logo appeared in the middle of the room, just floating there. A narrator's voice said, "Dinosaurs, Where are They Now?" while the phrase appeared in big block letters that hovered in space. Then, the entire landscape of the room changed and we found ourselves standing in a holographic representation of Earth, in the Jurassic Era. There were lush plants, towering trees, and vividly colored flowers in every direction. Many of the spectators tried to reach out and touch the surroundings, but their hands passed right through.

I was captivated. I caught Celeste peeking over at me, to see if I was enjoying myself. The grin plastered on my face told her I was. Suddenly, we heard a roar. It ripped through the theater like it was actually in the room with us. Little kids huddled close to their parents as we heard thumping and pounding. The ground started shaking and from out of the bushes came a gigantic, holographic Tyrannosaurus Rex.

I stood there, awestruck, as the prehistoric beast thundered across the planetarium. As it disappeared back into the movie screens, people started laughing, their fear turning to excitement. Everybody's eyes were glued open, as a hundred more dinosaurs came forward, filling the room. I saw velociraptors and Stegosauruses and, up in the sky, large, swooping Pterodactyls.

"As most of you know," said the narrator, "Dinosaurs originally came from Earth, where they roamed freely during the Jurassic Era. Dinosaurs were the planet's dominant species, formidable predators, both powerful and intelligent. But one question has plagued the universe for ages — what happened to them? For the people of Earth, the fate of the dinosaurs remains a mystery to this day. Some say they simply killed each other off..."

Suddenly, the holographic dinosaurs started fighting with each other. Brachiosauruses rammed Spinosauruses. Triceratopses stabbed Spinosauruses. And the mighty T-Rex stomped across the entire scene, crushing everything in sight.

"But this is an incorrect theory. While in-fighting certainly killed a great number of dinosaurs, it was not the reason for their sudden disappearance from Earth. Another theory suggests that a meteor struck Earth, killing all life on the planet..."

A holographic comet came flying towards us. The flaming fireball passed right through the crowd, with a loud explosion.

"This, however, is also incorrect. In truth, nothing killed the dinosaurs. They're still alive."

Many people, including myself, gasped. Still alive? There was no way. The Akashic Records had to be wrong. If dinosaurs were still on Earth, somebody, somewhere, would have discovered them. Right?

"The fact of the matter is Earth was indeed struck by a massive meteor. But several days before this catastrophic event occurred, a rescue mission was launched by the Endangered Species Coalition."

Holographic beings showed up, wearing silver spacesuits and protective goggles. My face contorted in confusion. The who?

"The Endangered Species Coalition," explained the narrator, "has rescued almost 100 species from across the galaxies, saving them from endangerment and extinction. When they heard that a powerful meteor was on course to strike the planet Earth, and kill every remaining dinosaur, the E.S.C. sprung into action. With monetary contributions from across the galaxy, the Coalition built a fleet of cargo ships and flew to planet Earth in one of history's most impressive rescue missions."

All around us, massive ships began to descend from the sky, landing in the lush foliage. Their cargo doors opened and hundreds of beings in silver spacesuits scurried out. Using advanced equipment, they began herding the dinosaurs into the ships, one by one, including the mammoth T-rexes. I watched the fate of the dinosaurs unfold before my very eyes.

After the last dinosaur was packed onto the last ship, the entire fleet took off and the narrator resumed.

"The E.S.C. arrived just in the nick of time. Within days of this rescue mission, a meteor smashed into Planet Earth, sending debris into the environment, rendering it unable to support dinosaur life. If not for the fast action and good will of the E.S.C., one of the galaxies' most fascinating species would have been eliminated. But instead, to our collective benefit, dinosaurs are still alive, most of them living peacefully on the planet Dino in the Whirlpool Galaxy."

A final holographic representation showed thousands of dinosaurs grazing peacefully on a strange purple, landscape that was unfamiliar to me. Music began to play and the screens went blank. All the lights came up and the crowd applauded.

"Is that true?" I said to Ari and Celeste.

"Of course," said Ari. "You can even go on a safari and see them. We'll save that for your next trip."

After the theater, we spent a few minutes in the gift shop like all the other tourists and Celeste bought me a cool meteorite necklace as a souvenir. The little informational card attached to it said the stone was from the planet Pollux, in the Gemini system, and that it was actually considered to be a flint, because if you struck it against metal, it would make a spark. I don't really wear necklaces, but this one was pretty neat, and a present from Celeste, so I happily put it around my neck and left it there. We also bought three Globular Clusters from the cafeteria, the alien version of ice-cream, which I devoured in a minute flat.

All in all, it was easily the best museum I've ever been to and I would've done anything to stay there a few hours longer. But Celeste put her foot down. We'd pressed our luck and she was done showing me outer space. Yes, initially, they had bigger plans for me, including a trip to the Universe Mall on Beta Librae and a visit to an intergalactic Zoo in the Eagle Nebula. But Celeste was convinced the authorities were on to us and she wanted to get me back to Earth as soon as possible. Besides, I knew my family back home was probably worried sick about me. And so even though Ari tried to convince me that I should see a few more sights, I ultimately sided with Celeste — it was time to bring my alien adventure to an end.

Chapter 6 BACK TO EARTH

An hour later, I was zoned out in the backseat of their spaceship, processing everything I'd seen and done in outer space. And that was a lot. I had flown to the furthest reaches of the galaxy, seen almost every planet in our Solar System, set foot on two foreign worlds, and met a bunch of cool people, some human, some not. But of all the things I experienced on my journey, the one thing I couldn't get out of my head was that statue of Andromeda Aldebaran. Her resemblance to my mother was simply uncanny and so finally I decided to ask Ari and Celeste for more information about her.

"You're lucky," said Celeste. "I did a book report on Andromeda Aldebaran in the fifth grade. I'm kind of an expert on her life. What do you wanna know?"

"Anything," I said. "Everything."

"Well, one thing's for sure," said Celeste. "Being from Earth, she tried desperately to get you guys into the League of Planets. Remember, we told you all about the League earlier? The governing body of the universe?"

I nodded, indicating that I was following her.

"Well, Andromeda Aldebaran would go around giving

speeches, trying to prove that Earthlings were ready to learn about extraterrestrial life and should be welcomed into the League of Planets. She said most Earthlings were good people, compassionate and caring and ready to help others in need. But it never went over. There was just too much resistance by close-minded snobs like my brother here who feel that Earthlings aren't advanced enough."

"Hey, have you seen some of the human beings down there?" said Ari, shuddering.

Celeste and I ignored him.

"What about her husband," I asked. "What was his name?"

"Atlas Aldebaran!" said Ari, jumping in. "He was like the most amazing military hero ever. Now we're on a topic I know something about."

Celeste shrugged.

"I'm not really into wars and stuff, but yes Atlas Aldebaran was a very decorated and accomplished fighter."

"He's saved lots of planets from invasion, including Earth," said Ari.

"The Earth was almost invaded?" I said, surprised.

"Oh, yeah. A few times," said Celeste.

"By who?" I said.

"Lots of different races. You've got a very valuable planet down there, Alan. Remember Earth is the home-planet for every human being in the universe. It's the planet of origin. A lot of people would love to control it."

A chill went through me. The idea that our planet had come under threat of invasion and nobody knew about it was terrifying.

"So let me ask you a question, Alan," said Celeste. "Why so curious about Andromeda Aldebaran? I mean you were acting pretty strange back there at the Akashic Records. It was like you recognized her or something."

Celeste had hit the nail on the head, but how could I tell them what I was thinking, that Andromeda Aldebaran resembled my mother?

"No reason," I said. "Forget it."

"Come on, something's up. I can practically read your mind by now," said Celeste.

"We've only known each for like a day," I said.

"Not to me," she said. "I've been listening to you on the radio for 8 months now, and I think I've gotten to know you. And that statue of Andromeda Aldebaran had an effect on you, Alan. I could tell instantly back at the museum. So

come on, you can trust me. What's going on in that little
Earthling brain of yours?"

I thought it over. Why not? Ari and Celeste were my
new friends, and my mother always taught me that if you
want to build a friendship with someone, you have to trust
them.

"Fine," I said, then took a measured pause, studying
them. "The things is... that statue looked exactly like my
mother."

My words hung in the air for a long time. They
both seemed shocked. I immediately regretted opening my
mouth.

"Ooookay," said Ari, unsure of how to react.

"It's true," I said.

"Alan, a lot of people feel that way about Andromeda
Aldebaran. She's so awesome that by nature, you want to be
connected to her in some way. When I was younger I thought
Dr. Aquarius Farholm was my long lost grandfather. But
it's just a psychological phenomenon — it's called projection
or something."

"Hey, I'm not crazy," I said, a little insulted. "You
asked me why I was acting so weird back there at the
museum and I'm telling you. She looked like my mom. I don't

care if you believe me or not."

They both went quiet.

"So you think... what?" said Ari. "Andromeda Aldebaran was your mother, and let me guess Atlas Aldebaran was your father? And when they weren't busy up here in outer space, saving the universe, they were down on Earth, in Kansas City, raising you and your sister!" He started cracking up. "It's absurd."

I shrugged and cocked my head, embarrassed.

"This is why I didn't want to tell you guys. I'm not saying that she is my mother, I'm just saying she looked like my mother, that's all. I don't know what it means."

Celeste didn't say much for a few minutes. Her eyebrows were tight, focused in concentration.

"What year were you born, Alan?" she said.

"1995," I said.

She stopped short and said, "Huh."

"What?" I said, studying her.

"That's around the time that Atlas and Andromeda disappeared from public life," said Celeste.

"Oh, come on," said Ari. "This is a ridiculous conversation."

"Just hang on a second," said Celeste. "What if, they retired from Intergalactic Politics because they were going to have a child? So they disappeared and went down to Earth to raise their kid. That would certainly explain why Alan's family has an Intergalactic Transceiver. I mean... it's not that crazy a theory, is it?"

"And Alan's their kid? Yes, it is crazy!" said Ari. He turned to me, mockingly. "Alan Aldebaran? What a pleasure to meet you. I'm Ari Einstein."

There was an awkward silence.

"Ari's right," I said. "Let's drop this."

"I am right," he agreed. "It's not healthy for you to think like this, Alan. Your parents are gone. I'm sorry to be so blunt, but I think it's a really bad idea for you to start entertaining thoughts that they might still be alive. You're making me feel guilty. I mean, us abducting you, bringing you up here into space, maybe it messed with your head a little. Maybe you're starting to think anything's possible, and so you're coming up with this crazy theory that your parents are still—"

Suddenly, the ship started beeping. It was a fast-paced warning sound, like an alarm, quickly bringing our conversation to an end, which was fine with me. It was getting a little too personal.

"What's happening?" I asked.

Celeste spun her pilot's chair around and studied the dashboard.

"Rear detection system," she said. "We're being followed. I knew it, I knew it, I knew it..."

"Keep your cool, Celeste. How far away are they?" said Ari.

"4 parsecs and gaining," she said. "They'll be on us in a few minutes."

"How do you know they're following us?" I said. "Maybe they're just passing through."

"We're in the Beta sector, deep in Ursa Minor," said Celeste. "Nobody passes through here, unless they're headed to Earth, like us. It's the E.P.A. They're here for us. I can just feel it."

"So what do we do?" I said.

"Um, that's easy," said Ari. "We get the heck outta here."

Celeste thought about it and nodded her agreement.

"Ari's right. If we get caught, it'll be the end of our lives as we know it. Buckle in, you two."

I didn't need to be told twice. I quickly pulled the security belt around my waist.

"Alright, boys, hang on to your stomachs," said Celeste. "Warp speed in 5, 4, 3, 2, 1 — "

She jammed the throttle forward and then...

Nothing. We didn't blast off, didn't go plummeting downward, didn't zoom away. Instead, we kept on floating casually through space.

"What happened?" said Ari.

"I have no idea," said Celeste, sounding panicked. She did a quick check of all her gauges.

"Engines are operational. Air pressure is sound. Warp drive seems totally fine. I don't get it."

"Uh, we have a problem," said Ari, pointing our attention back to the monitor. The mammoth ship that was following us was now much closer. "I think they've got us in a tractor-beam."

"Let's see if I can break loose," said Celeste.

She flipped a toggle and was about to give it another go, when suddenly, we heard a shrill, piercing noise. We all winced and covered our ears. It was deafening. The noise warbled through different phases, like a radio changing channels, trying to find the right station. It sounded like birds chirping then static then a dial-up modem and then finally we heard a voice. It was human, speaking English, but with a creepy, drawn out, quality.

"Attention passengers of Alpha Centauri Cruiser 1811. Do not be alarmed. Your ship has been immobilized. Escape is impossible. We are taking you to the planet Gravis, in the Zeta Reticuli system. Any resistance will be dealt with swiftly and harshly. We have complete control of your ship."

The line went dead.

"Who was that, Celeste? The E.P.A.?" said Ari.

But Celeste just sat there, her mouth wide-open.

"It's not the E.P.A.," she said.

"Then who?"

"Didn't you hear? The Zeta Reticuli system?"

"I don't know my geography like you! Who is it?"

Celeste waited a moment and then said:

"The Grays."

Chapter 7. THE GRAYS

"Who, or what, are The Grays?" I said.

Ari and Celeste were silent for a minute and then Celeste unloaded on Ari.

"I can't believe this is happening!" she said. "It's all your fault, Ari! I told you we should have taken Alan back to Earth hours ago!"

"Guys... talk to me... who are they?"

Ari finally took his eyes off the monitor, letting out a deep breath.

"The Grays are pure evil, bro. They're the villains of the universe."

"And what do they want with us?"

Ari studied me.

"Not 'us'," he said.

"me?" I said and he nodded. "Why?"

They both stayed silent.

"Why?!" I demanded. "What are they gonna do to me?"

"Tests," said Ari.

A shiver of fear went through me when he said the word and I was speechless. Celeste started to talk, mainly I think just to calm me down.

"The Grays are descendants of one of the original 7 colonies from Earth, Alan," she said. "They were humans who lived in Atlantis 10,000 years ago. Just like our ancestors, they fled Earth when the Great Flood came. But something happened to this particular group of colonists when they settled on their new planet. The environment there, it changed them. There was too much moonlight, not enough sunlight. And they became, well, Gray. They're all hairless and creepy now."

"Their planet deformed them," said Ari. "Now they're angry that they left Earth in the first place and they want it back."

"But more than anything," said Celeste, "Even more than going back to Earth, The Grays want to look human again," said Celeste. "So they abduct Earthlings every chance they get. They do tests on you guys, trying to figure out how they can return their DNA to normal. Only, it's not easy to abduct an Earthling, so they don't get many test subjects."

"They must have found out we had you up here in space and decided to take you off our hands," said Ari.

"I don't want to be experimented on by an alien race!" I said.

There was an awkward silence.

"I'm sorry, Alan," said Celeste. "We didn't mean to get you into this."

"Just get me out of it, and I'll forgive you," I said.

They both went silent, and I immediately felt doomed. I turned and stared out the window at the passing stars and suddenly had an overwhelming feeling of homesickness. How did this happen? I got dizzy, like I was in a dream. And then suddenly I realized that the ship was rocking back and forth.

"What's happening?" I said.

Celeste motioned out the front windshield.

"Black Holes," she said.

I peered out the front windshield to see dozens of large, dark spots littered across space, like stingrays.

"It's the Grays' natural defense system. You'd have to be crazy to attack them here."

Suddenly, our ship began to descend. We plunged downward, heading for a pale, colorless planet below us. As we penetrated the atmosphere and drifted down towards the surface, I saw towering craggy mountains and vast valleys filled with gray dirt. There were no signs of vegetation anywhere, no trees, no grass, no plants — no life.

It was bleak and barren, the most depressing place I had ever seen.

Our ship was no longer in our control, and yet somehow, it managed to land all by itself, gently touching down in a deserted valley.

"Exit your vehicle immediately," boomed a voice from the radio.

"What should we do?" said Celeste.

"Do we have a choice?" said Ari.

Celeste glanced at me, frowning.

"I'm so sorry, Alan."

She shut down the engines and lowered the ramp. Helpless, we stood up and walked out onto The Gray Planet.

The first thing to hit me was the stench. It was the most noxious smell I'd ever smelled, and that's coming from a kid who grew up around a lot of horse manure. I grabbed the collar of my shirt and pulled it over my nose. Ari and Celeste did the same, gagging, as we strode across the dusty, gray surface.

"Ugggh, what is that?!" I said.

"Sulfur mines," Celeste gasped, pointing at a bunch of caves imbedded in the cliff-sides. "The Grays use it as a power source."

Suddenly, we heard a grinding noise come from a looming mountain before us. A door opened up in the mountain's base, like a garage door, revealing a vacuous cave. And from out of that cave, walked The Gray Queen.

Now, if you want a detailed description of what a Gray looks like, you can research the accounts of Arthur J. Lindecott and Emma Garson, from Louisiana, who expertly described their appearance in their 1995 report to the Federal Government. But to my knowledge, no one else has gotten it quite right. And since I can't do Arthur and Emma's report any better, for now I'll just sum up the Grays appearance in two words: slender and bony. Slender legs, bony arms, slender necks, bony fingers. Really bony fingers. The kind that I still have nightmares about. Slender and bony are the two words that always come to mind when I think of them. And of course the third is, Gray. They're completely gray, from head to toe, the color of a rainy day.

The Queen strode down the long runway and then stopped directly before me. She seemed to be staring at me with wonder. Slowly, she extended a bony hand and touched my face. I recoiled in horror as her corpse-like fingers brushed the side of my cheek.

"What an honor it is to meet you," she said.

I didn't know how to reply as she stood there blinking at me, her enormous black eyes popping out of her bulbous, bald head. Her eyes were so big and piercing that I thought she could see down to my very soul. As she looked me over, a smile crept over her narrow lips, riding up the contours of her oval face.

"You don't know how much trouble we've gone through to find you, Orion."

Suddenly, my heart leapt. Orion? Did she say Orion? Maybe she had made a mistake...

"My name's not Orion," I said.

The Gray Queen grinned.

"Oh, but it is."

"No, it's not," I said. "My name's Alan Albright, from Kansas City, Earth."

"You've got the wrong kid," said Ari, laughing uneasily. "This was all just a big misunderstanding!"

The Gray Queen started to laugh — no, let me rephrase that — she started to cackle. A high pitched, unnerving squeal, like a witch.

"You're very amusing, young Centauri. Which is why I am going to let you and your sister go back into your ship and return to your planet. Give my regards to your father, the Senator."

"You know our father?!" said Ari, surprised.

"But of course. One of the few members of the League of Planets whom I actually respect."

Celeste stepped forward and bowed her head, courteous.

"Please, your highness, let Alan come with us. Our dad would be thankful for any kindness you show us. Just let us go, all of us, and I'm sure he'll reward you in some way."

"You have your father's tact and grace, young lady. But unfortunately, I cannot let young Orion here leave the planet. I've waited so long to have him as my guest."

"But my name's not Orion!" I said.

"Oh, but it is," she said. "Whether you realize it or not my dear boy, you are Orion Aldebaran."

My memories of the events that happened immediately thereafter are pretty hazy, but this much I know for sure: The Gray Queen did something to me. Right after she dropped the bomb about my true identity, I felt a sharp pinch in my shoulder and I passed out.

There is one thing I remember vividly though — at

some point I opened my eyes and saw several Grays looming over me, like surgeons, backlit by a halo of powerful lighting. I heard an evil voice whisper, "He's still awake," and then I felt a mask placed over my mouth and I fell asleep again.

Darkness... and then light... and then darkness again... Finally I opened my eyes to see that I was lying in a hospital bed, in some kind of underground laboratory. It took a moment for my pupils to adjust to the light, but when they did, I realized that I wasn't alone. The Gray Queen was beside me, seated in a chair, as if she had been watching me sleep. I gasped when I saw her, which I'm sure you could understand. It's a strange thing to wake up and find an alien staring at you.

"Ah, he lives," said The Queen. "You had me worried, Orion. I wasn't sure you were going to survive."

"What did you do to me?" I said.

"Nothing that would harm you, long-term. However, the experiments were painful enough that we felt it best to put you to sleep."

It suddenly dawned on me that my arms and legs were sore.

"What kind of experiments?" I said.

"Genetic," she said. "You're a very special child. We wanted to learn as much about you as possible."

"Where are my friends?" I said.

"The Senator's children? I let them go, as promised. I have no interest in starting a war with a politician. I returned them to their ship, and sent them on their way. Don't feel betrayed. I gave them little choice."

I swallowed hard, scared. For the first time in my outer space adventure I was on my own.

"Eat," said the Queen, placing a tray over my lap, like I was a patient in a hospital. "You must be hungry. Most Earthlings are, after they come out of testing."

I looked down at the tray she set before me and almost gagged. It was some kind of grilled creature, smothered in a sulfur sauce. There was a foul, putrid smell wafting off the dish, like burnt eggs.

"Now don't offend me, Orion," said The Queen.

I decided that anything I could do to get in the Queen's good graces would probably be helpful to me in the long run. And so, without giving it too much thought, I bit my lip and held my breath and decided to take the plunge. I'd seen enough reality TV shows to know that eating disgusting food was simply a case of mind over matter.

Humans can eat all kinds of things, from tarantulas to frogs' guts to whatever, and I'm using those examples because that's how gross this thing looked. It was like a large larvae, or a maggot, the size of a loaf of bread, with sharp teeth. But who knows, some things taste a lot better than they smell.

This thing didn't. I nervously cut into the dead wormy creature, then raised the utensil to my mouth and ate it. I didn't even try to chew it. I just wanted to get it down and so I practically swallowed it whole. The Queen smiled at me and clasped her hands together, like I had passed some kind of test. She was pleased with me, I could tell, and so even though I was ready to puke, I was happy with my choice to go for it.

"You're very brave," said The Queen. "And courteous. I would expect nothing less from the son of Atlas Aldebaran."

I stared at her.

"Is he really my father?"

"But of course. Don't you know it already, deep down?"

I went quiet. She was right. I did know it. The mysteries of my life were coming together, like the scattered pieces of a puzzle.

"Is he alive?" I asked.

"He's alive, and he's here."

My heart leapt in my chest.

"And my mom?" I said.

"Your mother, I'm sorry to say, is no longer with us."

My heart sank as I studied the Queen.

"Did you kill her?"

The Queen flashed a despicable grin.

"Not exactly, no."

"What's that mean?"

"Let's not get into the specifics of Andromeda Aldebaran's demise. She was a wonderful woman, proud and true, and the universe will remember her that way."

As I fought back tears, she suddenly stood up, clutching a goblet in her bony white fingers.

"Tell me, Orion, is it really true that you've known nothing about your true identity? All this time on Earth, your parents never told you a single thing?"

I shook my head.

"So all the while, they were leading two separate lives. Up here they were Atlas and Andromeda Aldebaran, perhaps the most famous duo in the universe; while down on Earth they were—"

She looked at me, wanting me to complete the sentence.

"Derek and Karen Albright," I said.

"Derek and Karen Albright, yes," she said, laughing. "Do you know how long I searched for your parents? How many planets I scoured? Of course The Earth was an obvious choice for their retirement, but it's a very difficult planet to access, especially for us Grays. A shame, isn't it? The Earth used to be our home, yet now we aren't allowed anywhere near it."

I didn't know what to say, so I stayed quiet. She waved her hand in a circle, as if there were no point in talking 'politics' with me.

"In any case, it wasn't until last year that we finally managed to pinpoint your parents location and abduct them. You were told they were killed?"

I nodded.

"I suppose we could have abducted you and your sister as well, kept the whole family together. But we decided to let you be. Abducting children isn't our nature. However, imagine my surprise when you came into outer space of your own accord, well that was another story, wasn't it? Then, you were fair game. Then, I almost felt it was my <u>responsibility</u> to find you, to bring you here, to reunite you with your father."

"When can I see him?" I said.

"After dinner," said The Queen, grinning.

I stared down at my plate, held my breath and started to eat.

After consuming the most disgusting meal of my entire life, the Gray Queen helped me out of bed and led me down a dark and twisting tunnel that burrowed deep into the heart of her underground lair. Long, sharp stalactites hung from the ceiling and strange rodents scurried past my feet. I felt something whisk by my head that was the size of a bat and buzzed like a bumblebee. It was the creepiest place I'd ever been in in my life, but I didn't care. All I could think about was whether or not The Queen was telling the truth. Was my dad really here, a prisoner for the last year?

After a million twists and turns, we came to a futuristic-looking door imbedded in a rock wall. There was a Gray guard standing beside it with a laser-gun holstered to his hip. The Queen nodded and the guard pressed a glowing button and the door went zipping upward at lightning fast speed, revealing a dimly lit prison cell.

Sitting there on the other side, huddled beneath a blanket, was my father.

Chapter 8.   ATLAS ALDEBARAN

It took me all of three seconds to get over the shock of my dad's appearance — he had a big full beard and long straggly hair — before I went rushing forward into the cell and crashed into him, throwing my arms around him and hugging him as tight as I could. He was of course as equally stunned as I was, if not more, and so for a good 30 seconds, neither of us spoke. We just sat there, holding each other, and yes, crying. I can't explain what it feels like to find out that someone you thought was dead is alive.

Finally my father pulled back and clasped my head between his hands and just looked at me. We stared into each others' eyes and both of us started to laugh.

"Am I dreaming?" he said.

I shook my head, grinning from ear to ear.

"I knew you didn't die in that car accident!" I said. "I never believed it."

"How did you get here?" he said, turning to the Queen. "You abducted my son? Even you wouldn't pull something like this, Desdemona—"

The Queen sighed, raising a hand.

"Of course I wouldn't. You know me better than that, Atlas. Your son was brought into space by two children from the Alpha Centauri system. They abducted him, not me."

"Alpha Centaurians?" said my dad, turning to me.

"It was my fault dad. I used your radio. The one in the barn."

My dad's eyes went wide as he put the pieces together.

"And they picked up the transmissions?"

I nodded.

"A boy and a girl my age. They were curious about me, so they came down and took me. They wanted to show me outer space."

"So you see," said The Gray Queen. "I've done nothing wrong. All I did was help Orion find his way to you. I've reunited you with your one and only son, Atlas. You should be thrilled!"

But my dad didn't look thrilled.

"I want you to send him home. Now."

"Dad, no, I don't want to leave."

My dad kept his eyes focused on The Gray Queen.

"This is a violation of every intergalactic protocol in existence. You can't keep him here."

"I can't?" said The Gray Queen.

She started to laugh, pacing the cell.

"Look at it through my eyes, Atlas. As long as I have been Queen, you have been my biggest adversary. Now, of course, like all my adversaries, you eventually lost. You are my prisoner, and your wife has suffered a terrible fate. But what of your children? Orion knows the truth now. What's to stop him from growing up, becoming a powerful warrior just like his father, and exacting his revenge upon me? Wouldn't I be a fool to let him go?"

"You'd be a fool not to let him go," said my dad.

"Are you threatening me?"

"Yes," said my dad, staring daggers at her.

The Gray Queen grinned. It was clear that they had a long history that I knew nothing about.

"I'll tell you what," said The Queen. "I'm going to sleep on it. Tonight, enjoy your time together. Catch up with each other. After all, you haven't had any communication for an entire year. I'm sure you have a lot to talk about. Come tomorrow, I will have decided both of your fates."

She headed for the door, then stopped and glanced

back at us one last time.

"But I should tell you, I'm leaning towards killing you both."

She cackled wickedly and exited the cell.

The minute she was gone, my father moved closer to me, his voice changing back to the fatherly tone I'd always known.

"Are you alright?" he said.

I nodded.

"Son... You need to know... your mother..."

"I know, dad," I said. "The Queen told me."

He pulled me closer and said, "I'm sorry."

"I just can't believe this, any of it," I said.

I trailed off, unable to speak — everything caught up with me at once, all my emotions, and like a computer without enough RAM, my brain crashed. I pulled back and just sat there, staring at my dad with a blank expression. His eyes told me he completely understood.

"I know. You have a million questions. And I'm going to explain everything, I promise."

"Is my name Alan Albright or not?" I said.

"That's your Earth name. Just like mine is Derek and your mother's was Karen. We had to give ourselves fake identities in order to stay hidden from our enemies. But your outer space name is Orion."

"What's Katie's outer space name?"

"Aurora."

Out loud, I said each of the names one time, rolling them on my tongue: Atlas, Andromeda, Orion, and Aurora. I started smiling, because I liked them all. They just felt right.

"Your mother and I always wanted to tell you the truth, but we were never sure how or when to do it. We were going to tell you when you were 10, and then we thought, no, wait until he's older, and then we thought when you were 11... but we just couldn't bring ourselves to shock you like that... and then... well then we were abducted. The Grays came to Earth and snatched us right out of our car. You can't imagine how helpless we felt. Our old enemies finally caught up with us, our biggest fear had come true. And we never got to say goodbye to our children, never got to explain the truth..."

I just sat there, listening, captivated.

"You know those research trips I used to take?"

"Yeah?" I said.

"That was a cover. I wasn't going to other farms. I

was going to other planets. The truth is I've been operating in secret, running missions as Atlas Aldebaran all throughout your childhood."

My jaw fell open.

"I never stopped working. And that's why the Grays abducted me. I was about to foil their newest plan, their most sinister one yet," he said.

"What plan?"

"They want to destroy our sun, Alan," he said.

"How could they do that?"

"They've built a machine that can generate a black hole. And they're going to use it to create one in our solar system so big, it would swallow the sun."

I went silent, horrified by the thought.

"Almost every living thing on Earth would perish. The only species capable of surviving there would be one that doesn't need sunlight..."

My eyes went wide.

"Like The Grays," I said, understanding.

My dad nodded.

"That's right. Once everyone on Earth is gone, The Grays will move in. Do you know what a Quasar is?"

I shook my head and my dad made a circle with his thumb and forefinger.

"It's a galaxy with a supermassive black hole at the center, instead of a sun. If the Grays succeed, that's what will happen to the entire Milky Way. Our sun will disappear, and there will be a black spot so big in the center of the galaxy, it will become a quasar."

"They captured me because I know about the black hole generator," he continued. "It's here. On this planet. A giant machine the size of a football field, and I was coming here to destroy it. But they found me first. Somehow they learned that your mother and I were in Kansas City and they took us."

He paused, taking a deep breath.

"And this is where I've been for the past year, stuck in this cell, helpless, knowing that any day, the Earth might be destroyed... and that you... and Katie..."

He trailed off, staring at me.

"How is she?" he said.

"The same, I guess," I said. "The night I was abducted was the night of her 9th birthday party."

I guess the simple thought of my sister having a birthday was enough to make my dad pretty emotional, because he suddenly raised his hands to his eyes, wiping tears again.

"I prayed every night that I'd see you one more time," said my dad.

"Me too," I said.

We hugged again. And then, as my dad pulled back, I realized he was grinning.

"You know, much of what happens in life is predestined, Alan. Do you know what that word means?"

I shook my head.

"It means that all of this was meant to be: you being abducted, you coming here, to the Gray Planet, finding me -- it was all written in the stars."

"I don't understand, dad."

"Let me show you."

Suddenly, he yanked aside the blanket he had been sitting on, revealing a big ball of dirt that had been compacted together, like a mud pie.

"A few months ago, I found traces of Sulfur and Potassium Nitrate in the dirt floor of my cell, two highly explosive minerals. I've been gathering as much of them as I could. It's a bomb, Alan."

My eyes went wide, and I realized instantly --

"You're trying to escape!" I said.

"Of course I'm trying to escape. I'm an Aldebaran."
He picked up the ball of mud.

"It's been ready for almost two weeks now, but I've had no way of igniting it. I needed a spark. And now, here you are, and you've brought me one."

What spark? What was he talking about? I was totally confused at first. But then my dad pointed at my neck and I realized what he was getting at. I was wearing the flint necklace that Celeste had bought me at the Akashic Records!

"The universe works in mysterious ways, son."

He stuck out his palm and I removed the necklace from around my neck, handing it over. He held it up to the light.

"I'll answer all of your questions as soon as we're safe. But for now, what do you say we get out of here?"

*   *   *   *   *

A few seconds later, my dad scraped the flint across the metal surface of the door, got some sparks, lit the bomb and then huddled over me in the corner of the cell, covering my body. There were a tense few seconds, and then — KABOOM — I felt the heat from the massive explosion as the door was blown right off its hinges, sending the guard outside flying through the air. He crawled on the floor, trying to reach his laser pistol, but my father was quicker, leaping out of the cell, kicking the Gray clean across the jaw.

My dad scooped up the unconscious alien's laser gun and grabbed my hand and we took off running. It was a panicky run, and I assumed he didn't know where we were going, just that we had to keep moving, and so I did.

We rounded a corner and came headlong into a group of Gray soldiers who must have heard the explosion. The moment they saw us, they opened fire. We ducked back around the corner as blue laser bolts went zipping behind our necks, missing us by inches. I thought we were going to retreat in the other direction, but much to my surprise, my father leapt back out into the corridor, right into the maelstrom of fire and started shooting back

Seeing my dad dodging a hail of laser fire, ducking, crouching, and firing back, like some kind of big-screen action hero, I put all my previous conceptions of him to rest. Derek Albright from Kansas City died for me for real at that moment, replaced by Atlas Aldebaran. After causing The Grays to slow their advance, he came racing back around the corner, pulling me forward.

"How do you know where you're going?" I said.

"I've escaped from here before. I was a P.O.W. in the Syrian-Gray wars for a good two months before I finally managed to break out."

"How?"

"The Sulfur mines. If we can get to the mines, we can make it outside."

"And how do we get to the mines?" I asked, trying to keep up with him.

"Just follow your nose," he said.

And then I realized he was leading us in the direction of the foul smell of Sulfur. I had picked up faint traces of it here and there, but I didn't know my dad was actually using the scent to guide us.

After a few more twists and turns, we finally reached The Gray's sulfur mine. It was a gargantuan, vacuous cave, but it might as well have been a giant toilet bowl, that's how disgusting the smell was.

There were alien workers everywhere, digging into the rocky earth with pick-axes, chipping chunks of Sulfur off the walls, and placing the dirt into mine carts, which cruised along railroad tracks that lead right out of the cave's mouth.

The smell was overpowering.

"Oh, man," I said, nearly barfing.

"Just hang in there. We're almost out."

We stayed concealed in the shadows, as my dad surveyed the scene.

"We have to take the mine carts," he said.

My eyes followed the parade of bins as they rolled past, like roller coaster cars. Each one was filled with chunks of sulfur. Before I could even put up an argument, my dad grabbed me, lifted me up and tossed me right inside one of the carts. Then he jumped over the lip and joined me.

It was like being thrown into a dumpster. Even worse. Like being thrown into a big pile of horse —well, you get the picture. I've spelled it out enough. It stunk. And to make matters worse, we had to duck down and cover ourselves with the stuff. Before I knew it, I was buried in chunks of sulfur.

I could feel our mine cart coasting along, as my heart pounded in my chest. My eyes were closed tight. The sulfuric rock was all over me. My anxiety was at an all time high. And then, it happened -- my hyperventilation kicked in, and I suddenly felt like I was going to suffocate. I could feel my father's hand on mine, trying to comfort me, but have you ever been buried alive? I wasn't easily comforted. And so while I'm not proud of what happened next, I certainly can understand it, looking back:

I poked my head up. Yeah, I know, it was completely stupid. But I couldn't help it. I shot up and gasped for breath, sending a pile of rocks tumbling out of the mine cart. The movement was enough to attract the attention of a handful of Gray workers, who immediately stopped what they were doing and stared at me, stunned.

At first, they didn't react. I suppose the sight of a human boy riding along in their mine carts would be like an alien appearing on a conveyer built in an auto factory in Detroit. Just so surreal, that The Grays couldn't even grasp it for a moment. But then their instincts kicked in, and they started screaming. This attracted the attention of their supervisors, who drew laser guns and started firing.

My dad quickly popped up beside me, blaster drawn, shooting back.

"Get down!" he shouted.

The barrage of lasers swarmed past us, singeing the metallic cart and frying the sulfuric rocks. My dad fired away, but we were pressing our luck. I just had this horrible feeling that at any moment, one of us was going to get shot. Our little mine car rolled towards the cave's mouth. I never wanted to reach a destination so badly. 20 yards. 10 yards. Just a few more feet...

And then we got hit. Not me, not my father, but our mine cart. It took a direct blast to the wheels, and just as we reached the literal 'light at the end of the tunnel' our little escape vehicle was blown clean off the tracks.

We went flying out of the mine shaft, off-kilter, our cart soaring through the air for a few moments, before landing on the side of the mountain. I was thrilled we had made it out of the cave, but we were now sliding down a cliff at top speed, in a hard, metallic cart, and there was no way to stop it. Our fate was sealed. There were all sorts of rocks and boulders at the base of the mountain, and I had visions of smashing into them at top speed, and well... dying. That would be that. I had been through some serious trials and tribulations up 'til now, but this was the first time that my life actually flashed before my eyes. I saw myself as a child, riding Peanut Butter and Jelly; I saw me and Katie arguing over the TV remote control; I saw me and Andy Weiner building our treehouse in the forest; I saw a thousand images in rapid succession as we went sliding the mountain at top speed. And then —

Boom! We hit something. The mine cart came to an abrupt stop, turned over, and I was thrown through the air with my father. We landed practically on top of each other, and although I was hurt, I was pretty sure I was still alive. I looked up, wincing, to see my father scrambling to his feet beside me.

"Are you alright?" he said, placing an arm around me. I managed to say yes, and he started pulling me along.

"The runway... can you make it?"

Up ahead was the Gray's enormous military-like airport, filled with rows and rows of spaceships. I nodded and we started sprinting for it. I've never run so fast in my life. I glanced back over my shoulder to see an army of Grays following us, pistols out, firing lasers. We hit the hard concrete of the landing strip and started making our way towards one of the sleek, disc-shaped UFO's. My dad approached the nearest one and tapped a control panel on the underbelly of the ship. Instantly, a ramp lowered.

"Get in!" he said.

I didn't hesitate, scurrying up the ramp.

"Do you know how to fly these?" I asked him.

"There's not a ship in the universe I can't fly," said my dad. As I looked back at him, I remember being flooded with a warm feeling of security and confidence that somehow we were going to make it out of this...

Unfortunately, that feeling was immediately replaced by one of utter dread, as I watched my father drop to his knees, wincing. He let out a horrific scream and clutched his shoulder. It took me a moment to realize what had happened, but as he pulled his hand away, it was clear he had been shot in the shoulder. There was a smoking black hole in his shirt and the foul stench of burning flesh.

"Dad!"

He laid down in the belly of the ship, woozy.

"Are you alright?" I said, kneeling beside him. He tried to speak, but his face was contorted in pain. The last thing he managed to do was punch a button on the ship's wall, sealing it shut. And then, he pulled me close.

"Get us out of here," he managed to whisper.

"But I can't fly--"

"You can do anything, Orion," he said.

My dad closed his eyes and passed out.

Chapter 9. ORION ALDEBARAN

Through the front windshield, I could see a group of Gray aliens rushing towards the ship, firing laser beams. Shots ricocheted off the exterior, keeping us safe inside, but I knew it was only a matter of time before they reached the ship, lowered the ramp, came on board, and recaptured us. I knew what I had to do, but... me? Fly an alien ship? Celeste had given me a brief lesson on our departure from Earth, I mean I knew the basics, but to actually take off?

I nervously bit my lip and then took the pilot's seat. I placed my hands on the controls and studied the dashboard. There was an array of foreign controls, demarcated with unintelligible symbols. I scanned the dashboard and then did my best guess and pressed a round, green button directly in front of me.

Good guess. The entire ship came to life. The lights started flashing and I felt the gentle vibration of the engines. Okay. The steering wheel was just like the one of the videogames they have at the Kansas City mall. I could handle it. But the speed... where was the speed? How did I start this thing?

I pushed forward on a U-shaped throttle and got my

answer, as the ship suddenly went tearing off down the runway. I let out a startled gasp. I didn't know what I was doing, but I was moving!

I went rocketing past rows and rows of parked spaceships, as hundreds of Gray aliens took position and started shooting at me, like cops trying to stop a getaway car. But I had the luxury of cluelessness on my side, meaning I couldn't steer this thing and The Grays knew it. They went diving out of the way as I barreled forward, threatening to run them right over.

As I peered into the distance, I saw that I was running out of room. The airstrip was coming to an end, and up ahead there was nothing but a vast desert, filled with sand. I knew that I had to take off, I just didn't know how. I thought back to what Celeste had taught me. I needed to find the plunger. I saw a small, white knob protruding from the dashboard, just begging me to pull it. So I did.

Whoooosh! The ship immediately went swooping upward into the air and before I even knew what was happening I was flying. I couldn't help myself from letting out a loud, "Whoo-hoo!" I think the Grays were just as shocked as I was that I had pulled it off, because most of them stopped firing and just stood there on the runway, watching me, as I soared over their heads. A huge grin spread across my face. Up until this moment, the biggest risk I'd ever taken was riding Peanut Butter and Jelly at top speed through a Kansas City forest. But this was something else, a rush of energy that filled my entire body. I had done it!

And then, suddenly, I saw something looming in the canyon ahead. It was a giant, oval-shaped machine, the size of a football field, bigger than any machine I'd ever seen. It looked like some kind of powerful reactor and I just knew in my gut it was The Grays black-hole generator, the one my dad told me about. There it was, right in my sights -- I could destroy it!

Suddenly — BOOM. My ship got rocked by a laser blast. I looked back over my shoulder and saw a squadron of spinning disks flying through the sky like giant Frisbees, right on my tail. I turned back around and studied the dashboard. Where were the weapons systems? A missile, a laser-gun, anything...

I groped behind the steering wheel and felt two triggers where my index fingers were. I took a deep breath, squinted and then squeezed the triggers over and over. ZAP-ZAP-ZAP! Laser beams erupted from the underbelly of my ship, raining down on the black-hole generator. I didn't let up, squeezing my fingers non-stop, creating a rapid stream of lasers. Finally, I must have hit something important, because there was a deafening thunderclap and a mushroom cloud of fire erupted right beneath my ship. I hit the jets and sped forward as I felt the heat from the explosion warming up the hull.

There was a domino effect, the first blast triggering another and another, all of them detonating right below me, as the black-hole generator started to go up in flames. I turned to look out the rear window, witnessing a fireworks display like something out of a war movie. Orange fireballs filed the air, lighting up the black sky of the planet.

"Dad!" I screamed. "I did it!"

And then, I turned my eyes forward and saw the mountain. An enormous one, directly in front me, a flat sheet of rock that seemed to stretch up into the heavens. There was no way over it, no way around it, and if I didn't do something fast, I was going to crash right into it. It seemed to materialize out of nowhere, right in front of my eyes.

I grabbed the plunger and started pulling. I needed to ascend, right now. I struggled with all my might, but the plunger was resisting me. I tugged with every muscle, closing my eyes. I couldn't look.

And then, at the last second, my ship went completely

vertical and started scaling upward along the face of the mountain. I went shooting directly towards the atmosphere, at a 90 degree angle, like a rocketship.

I opened my eyes. I was looking straight at the stars. The dull, colorless sky of the Gray Planet gave way to the crisp blackness of space. The ship started vibrating so intensely I thought I was going to be sick. My hands could barely hold on to the controls. Just as I thought the pressure was going to be too intense and the ship was going to break apart... everything became calm.

I was in space, soaring across it like a comet. All the bouncing and jerking stopped and the ride became smooth. I had done it. I escaped from The Gray Planet!

"Dad!" I screamed, glancing back at him. "Dad! We're free! We made it!"

No sooner had I uttered this celebratory cry then my ship got completely rocked by a laser blast. I immediately grabbed the controls again and glanced down at the radar, which showed 6 beeping dots approaching, right on my tail. We had been followed, of course. I don't know what I was thinking. I should have known better than to think the Grays would let me escape without giving chase. They swarmed around me like hornets, moving in cross-cross patterns, firing at me with red lasers beams that tore across space.

Now, I did have one advantage. I was a kid who grew up on Earth in the age of technology, and I had played my share of videogames. My hand-eye coordination was stellar, and I wasn't about to sit in that pilot's seat without taking some kind of evasive action. And so, I started to pretend that I was in the arcade. I settled back in the chair, gripped the controls and focused my attention.

The first thing I did was push the plunger all the way forward, sending my ship into a sharp descent and sending my belly all the way up into my throat. Much to my surprise, however, I felt completely comfortable behind the wheel, like I could make a bunch of sharp turns and sudden moves without getting sick. And so that's exactly what I did.

As they swirled around me, I gave the Grays a good run for their money, evading all six of them. They were spinning through space at top speed, trying to keep up with me, but I was good. I made a sudden dip that threw them off completely, and as one of them opened fire, he miscalculated and wound up shooting one of his own comrades. I watched the enemy ship explode in a flash of blue and green flames, leaving only five Grays to deal with.

I started to think that I just might have a shot at escaping alive, when suddenly --

I lost control. I wasn't sure how. It wasn't like I had been hit with a laser blast. It was a different feeling. The ship just started slipping and sliding all across space, like a marble on a warped surface. I struggled with the steering wheel, totally confused, until I glanced out the front windshield and immediately understood --

The Black Holes. The ones we saw on our approach to The Gray Planet. They were looming just ahead of me, littered across space like giant blankets, as dark as night. And they weren't just sucking <u>me</u> in, either! Two of the Gray spaceships that were on my tail suddenly went shooting right past me, completely out of control, flipping end over end as the gravitational pull of the black holes pulled them in like a tractor beam. Suddenly, The Grays and I had a bigger threat to worry about and our space battle was put on temporary hold.

I can't even tell you how terrifying a Black Hole is up close. You can feel its power. I shuddered at the thought of what would happen to me if I didn't somehow break free of its pull. I'd heard stories in science class that nothing escapes a Black Hole, not even light, and that anything that gets caught in one immediately collapses under the pressure, exploding into millions of tiny pieces.

I watched as the two Gray spaceships suffered this fate, suddenly disappearing from sight, growing smaller and smaller, until they were entirely devoured by the looming black mass. Just like that, they were gone. And I was next.

Going on pure instinct, I spun my ship around, so that the tail end was facing the Black Hole. Then, I slammed the throttle forward as far as it would go. I felt the engines fire with everything they had, resisting the force that was pulling us backwards. But you know how when you press the gas pedal on a parked car, the engine roars like a lion, but you don't go anywhere? I mean, not that I've ever driven or anything, but my grandfather would sometimes sit with me in his old Cadillac after he'd given it a tune up, and he'd rev the engine, and look at me, and say, "You hear that? Can you hear that power?" Well, imagine that force multiplied by a hundred and you'll get some idea of the power that suddenly started ripping through my UFO.

But we simply weren't moving. The Black Hole didn't want to let us go. It was a tug of war. The ship started vibrating, and I got scared, just from the sheer power of it all, like I was sitting on a bomb ready to explode. The tension was too intense. Something had to give — either the ship or the Black Hole.

And then something did. The ship won. It somehow managed to break free of the grip of the Black Hole's gravitational field, and just like that, we went blasting forward like a bat from a cave, so suddenly and so quickly that I was slammed back against the pilot's seat. I felt the skin of my face rippling as I shot forward at an incredible speed, hurtling through space.

And of course, what was directly ahead of me? The three remaining Gray ships, hovering like vultures, waiting to see if I was going to make it out of the grip of the Black Hole. And I think they were just as amazed as me to see that I had escaped, and they simply had no time to react as I came barreling directly towards them like a boulder launched from a catapult. In fact, I didn't have time to react either, which was bad, because it suddenly dawned on me that I was going to crash into them. I remember actually seeing the stunned look on their faces through their windshields, as my spinning disc careened forward, out of control. Two of the ships managed to dart away at the last second, but the remaining one was a sitting duck. I smashed its front windshield with the edge of my ship, shattering the glass, causing the Gray alien inside to get sucked right out into space. Pilotless, his UFO went veering off course and disappeared into the dark recesses of space, and just like that, there were only 2 Gray ships left to deal with.

And those two weren't about to let up. I think the fact that I had single-handedly managed to do away with four of their buddies only made them angrier. They fired a relentless onslaught of laser beams from behind me as I zigzagged through space. I knew that in order to survive, I was going to have to defeat them. I mean, there was no home base I could run to, no resting spot, like in tag. How could there be? I was in the middle of space and I didn't have the first clue where I was headed. In order to get out of this, I was going to have to destroy those ships.

I glanced down at the radar and saw that the two remaining Grays were directly on my tail. If I wanted to take a shot at them, I was going to have to get them in my sights first. So I did something a little dangerous, something that could have gotten me killed — I slowed down, and the Gray ships went flying right past me, not expecting me to hit the brakes like that. Suddenly, I was behind them! Without even thinking I squeezed the triggers and watched a powerful laser bolt blast out of my ship, careen across space, and hit one of the Gray ships directly in the rear end.

There was a brilliant explosion of light as the ship blew apart. I felt a moment of euphoria, but then quickly realized that I had lost sight of the sixth and final Gray ship. Somehow, it had slipped away from me. Even my radar seemed confused, showing nothing in the proximity, no blinking dots, except for me. Had I gotten lucky? Did it fly off? Was it afraid to face me one-on-one? Just as I was entertaining the possibility that it was all over --

BOOM. I got slammed by a direct hit. Just like that, the ship flipped over and I went flying out of the pilot's seat. Smoke started pouring out of the dashboard and the glowing lights inside the hull immediately went out, replaced by a blinking, flashing red emergency light. Somehow the ship managed to stabilize itself and I climbed to my knees, wheezing. I felt something sticky dripping down my forehead and reached up to find that I was bleeding. I looked over at my father, who had been thrown clear across the hull. He was laying sprawled out on the floor, unconscious. I crawled to his side.

"Dad," I said. "Dad, wake up! I need you!"

I started to cry. I felt like death was in the ship with us. I felt like it was the end. As I looked out the front windshield, I saw the sixth and final Gray ship, hovering directly ahead of us, like a predator. It just floated in space for a moment, calmly, lining up its shot. It was over, and I knew it.

The strangest feeling came over me; it was a mysterious chill, combined with a calming peace. My dad had told me that this was my destiny. To come into outer space, to reunite with him one more time. And if this is how it was all supposed to end, I decided then and there that it was worth it. I had seen my father again, just like I had prayed I would every single night for the last year. I had gotten my wish, and if this was the price I had to pay for it, I was ready. So I closed my eyes.

I heard the explosion first, impossibly loud, filling my ears. And then I saw bright spots of yellow and red from behind my eyelids and I remember thinking, this is death. This must be it. But that thought was immediately followed by a much stranger one: exactly how am I hearing things, and seeing colors, if I'm dead?

I opened my eyes. I was still in the UFO, kneeling at my father's side, very much alive. Out the front windshield, floating there in space, I saw the remnants of the last Gray ship, bits and pieces of machinery drifting lazily across the stars, like it had just been blown apart.

And then I heard static. The ship's radio crackled.

"Alan?! Alan, are you okay?"

I couldn't speak. I recognized it instantly as Ari's voice.

"Alan, answer us!" came a second voice — Celeste.

Suddenly her spherical ship came soaring directly overhead. I saw them both inside the orb, waving at me through the windshield.

"Alan!" said Ari.

"He's okay!" said Celeste, hugging him.

I crawled forward to the dashboard. Physically wiped out, I barely managed to speak into the intercom.

"You came back for me?" I muttered.

"Are you kidding, bro?" said Ari. "We never left."

Chapter 10. POLARIS AND PROXIMA CENTAURI

A warm feeling flooded over me. I was saved. My friends had come through when I thought all hope was lost. I felt relief and gratitude and an overwhelming sense that I'd gotten extremely, impossibly, lucky. I glanced back at my father who lay there motionless on the spaceship's floor.

"Guys," I said. "My father's hurt."

"And by your father, just to be clear, you mean Atlas Aldebaran?" came Ari's voice.

I realized that although I'd known the truth about my history for a few hours now, Ari and Celeste still weren't sure what was going on.

"Yes," I said.

"And he's with you?" said Celeste.

"Yeah... we escaped together. But he got shot and now he's unconscious," I said.

Suddenly, I welled up with emotion. My father was hurt and we were light-years away from Earth. I felt helpless and homesick and in all my adventure I'd never wanted to get back to Missouri so badly, back to my house, to my sister, to my grandmother and grandfather who'd know what to do.

"We're in way over our heads here," said Celeste. "We gotta tell mom and dad what's going on."

"Are you crazy?" said Ari. "They'll ground us 'til infinity!"

"We need a parent, Ari! I'm done following your lead."

Her voice suddenly came through stronger, to me.

"Alan, follow me back to our house. Our parents should be getting home from vacation soon. We'll tell them everything that's happened, and they'll be able to help us.

"Are you sure?" I said.

"It's the right thing to do," said Celeste.

Honestly, I felt relieved - we did need a parent. And since my dad was passed out on the floor of the ship, we would have to rely on Ari and Celeste's.

Following Celeste's instructions, I pressed a button on the console of the Gray ship that looked like this and then another button that looked this ℓ, entering the planetary code for Alpha Centauri, and then boom, I was off and flying, the ship's autopilot rocketing me through deep space.

After a few hours of cruising, during which I retraced the entire alien adventure in my mind, I finally emerged from deep-space into the familiar binary star system of Alpha Centauri, the green-blue surface of New Atlantis filling up our view.

Celeste's voice crackled on the radio.

"Follow me around to the other side of the planet," she said.

We descended through the bright blue sky, flying over the Atlantean Ocean, until we reached a sprawling estate on the coastline. Celeste landed her orb on the front lawn and then coached me through the process of doing the same. My ship set down with a thud and I pressed the lever for the landing ramp and went running out.

"Alan!" said Celeste, emerging from her ship. She rushed forward and hugged me.

"Dude!" said Ari.

I pulled back from Celeste and high-fived Ari, who caught my hand and pulled it back and forth like a hacksaw.

"Orion Aldebaran... crazy! Girls are gonna gravitate to you like planets."

"Guys..." said Celeste. She pointed across the front lawn at a ship with black windows, like an intergalactic SUV.

"Mom and Dad are already home."

* * * * *

We opted to leave my father in the Gray spaceship because a) moving him might be dangerous, and b) it was going to be hard enough explaining everything to Mr. and Mrs. Centauri without carrying my father's unconscious body through the door.

"Let me do all the talking," said Ari, as we approached the front door. He put his palm to it and it slid open, revealing the inside of the house. Standing there in the glass-and-silver living room, talking to a flat-screen monitor in the wall, was a very pretty woman in her forties with long dark hair and tan skin. This was Proxima Centauri, Ari and Celeste's mom, and she seemed utterly panicked at the moment.

"—I appreciate that Estrella," she was saying. "And if you could have Devon call us back if he hears anything from any of his friends—"

Suddenly she turned and saw us.

"They're home!" she gasped, clicking off the wall monitor, running toward her kids. "Polaris, they're home!"

She reached Celeste first, hugging her.

"Where have you two been? We've been trying to contact you for hours!"

She hugged Ari.

"It's a long story," said Celeste.

"Then you better start talking," came a voice. I turned to see a serious-looking man with sharp features and eyes like black holes enter the living room. This was Senator Polaris Centauri, their father, and his presence was so domineering that I could see instantly why Ari was hesitant to come clean about abducting me. He looked like the type of dad who had dished out some punishments in his lifetime.

"So? Would you care to tell your mother and I why you haven't been answering your phones? Or do you want to keep us in suspense even longer?"

"Mom, dad—" said Celeste, but before she could finish, Senator Centauri gasped.

"What in the galaxies...?" he said.

"Polaris, what is it?" said Mrs. Centauri.

"Who is this?" he said, pointing at me.

I couldn't move. The Senator took a few steps toward me, his voice suddenly very low and serious.

"Look at me, son," he said.

I froze.

"Son, I'm not going to ask you again. Kindly look up at me, so I can see your eyes."

The Senator's glare was fixed on me and I gulped, understanding immediately that this was not a man to mess around with. Relenting, I raised my head. As I did Mr. and Mrs. Centauri went wide-eyed with shock. They were both utterly astonished. Mrs. Centauri actually looked like she might pass out.

"Good Heavens. You're— You're an Earthling!" she said.

The fascination that I saw in her eyes was somewhat welcoming, compared to what I saw in Mr. Centauri's eyes. It was the look parents get when they realize their children have just plunged them headlong into a major crisis. I could sense Mr. Centauri's mind racing, figuring out how it was possible that an Earthling kid was standing in his living room, and more importantly, what he was going to do about it.

"How did he get here?" he said.

"Dad, you're gonna have to bear with us—"

"Ari, you have three seconds. I want an answer. How did he get here?"

"We abducted him," said Ari.

"Oh..." I heard Mrs. Centauri whisper, as she leaned on the wall for support.

"When?" said Senator Centauri.

"Just last night, it's hasn't even been 24 hours. But dad listen, you don't understand—"

"Why would you do such a thing?"

"I know dad, I'm sorry, I know it looks bad for you career —"

"My career? Is that what you think I'm concerned about? You could have been killed out there! Earth is 4 light-years away!"

"Four point two, actually," said Celeste.

Mr. Centauri whirled on her.

"Don't think this is something to be proud of Celeste. It's not. Don't you know the E.P.A. monitors all traffic on and off of Planet Earth? They could have shot you down. They don't know you're just kids. You're lucky they didn't blast your ship out of the air."

He spun, addressing his wife.

"This is a disaster," said Polaris. "I'm going to have to talk to Galactic Immigration Services. Maybe we can keep this below the radar..."

"Dad—" said Celeste.

"Say no more!" he shouted at her, turning to me. "Son, I'm sorry you were spacenapped. On behalf of the government of Alpha Centauri, you have my sincere apologies."

I kept quiet.

"I assure you, we're going to get you home safe and sound."

"Dad, would you please just listen!"

"Celeste, I told you—"

Finally, Celeste just exploded, blurting out—

"His name is Orion and he's the son of Atlas and Andromeda Aldebaran and his father is outside right now, lying unconscious in a Gray starfighter that's parked on our front lawn."

Both parents went completely silent, trying to process what they'd just heard. Finally, Mrs. Centauri crossed the room and tapped a switch on the wall. The blinds to the living room snapped open to reveal a window that peered out onto the front lawn, and sure enough, sitting there in full view was the Gray spaceship.

"Actually, I'm not unconscious anymore."

We all turned to see my dad standing in the doorway.

It took about a minute before anyone in the room said anything, when finally, Mrs. Centauri spoke.

"Captain Aldebaran...?" she said.

"Yes, ma'am," said my dad, nodding to her, then to Mr. Centauri. "Senator, I apologize for dropping in on you like this."

Senator Centauri was speechless, and I suspected it was one of the few times the man was at a loss for words. You could see his mind racing, trying to make sense of the situation. Mrs. Centauri, however, was bursting with excitement, unable to suppress her smile.

"I just can't believe it," she said, "Captain Atlas Aldebaran, in our living room. You'll have to excuse me for being so blunt, Captain, but....we thought you were dead. The whole universe thinks you're dead!"

"And that's how I'd like to keep it, if it's alright with you," said my dad.

Mrs. Centauri suddenly noticed my dad's wound.

"You're hurt," she said.

"It's not as bad as it looks. If you survive them, laser beam wounds aren't very painful."

"You would know," said Mrs. Centauri. "The stories of

your wartime exploits are legendary."

"And greatly exaggerated," said my dad.

"I'm sorry," Senator Centauri finally said, his voice commanding the attention of the whole room. "Let me see if I understand this situation right. My children went to Earth and abducted a boy who just happens to be the son of one of the galaxies' most legendary military heroes? Isn't that rather coincidental?"

"No, dad," said Celeste. "We went and got Alan — Orion — because he was broadcasting on an intergalactic transceiver. That's part of why we were curious about him. We couldn't understand where he got it."

"Listen, Senator," said my father. "I understand the predicament I'm putting you in by being here. But the way I see it, we've both got a lot to lose if this situation goes public. Nobody needs to know that Ari and Celeste abducted Alan."

"I wholeheartedly agree," said Senator Centauri.

As he said it, he aimed his laser-like gaze at my dad. The two men seemed to have an understanding.

"Good," said my father. "Then why don't we all sit down and figure this mess out?"

*   *   *   *   *

We retired to the kitchen table, where my dad brought Mr. and Mrs. Centauri up to speed on our whole adventure, starting with his retirement 13 years ago, and ending with me, Ari and Celeste saving him from the confines of The Grays' underground prison. Needless to say, the Centauris were a little stunned to learn that their children had not only broken several major intergalactic laws, but also helped rescue a famous military hero from the clutches of the most nefarious race in the universe. They sat in silence for a few moments, trying to process the whole story.

"One thing I don't understand," Senator Centauri said. "How did the Grays find you in the first place?"

"Obviously we were betrayed," said my father. "Someone gave up our location."

"But who knew you were there?"

"I don't know. But I'm going to find out."

"And what about your revenge?" said the Senator. "Surely you can't let the Gray Queen get away with this."

"I just got back from that awful planet, Senator. I

lost a lot while I was there. I have no intention of returning any time soon," said my father.

"But they kidnapped your child — mine too! Nobody wants to get back at them more than me."

"Polaris," interrupted Proxima, "Captain Aldebaran has served his galaxy. He'll make up his mind about his future plans when he's ready."

She turned to my dad.

"I know how much you loved your wife, Captain. We all loved her. The healing process takes time. Do what you need to and perhaps in due course, you'll find the desire to officially return to the military."

"Perhaps," said my dad, like a gentleman. But I could tell he was getting annoyed. And the Senator could probably sense this too, since he finally just sighed, waving his hand, letting it go. Instead, he turned his sights on me.

"Well, then, what about young Orion here? Can we expect great things from him?"

"Alan is going back to Earth tomorrow," said my dad.

I looked at him, a little surprised.

"I am?"

"You're going to finish out your childhood the way your mother intended it. Then, when you're old enough... we can decide what your role will be in outer space."

"But how can you expect me to go back to Mrs. Peachtree's English class now?" I said.

"Alan, I know you've had a taste of adventure, but... this isn't a game. We got very lucky to escape from the Gray Planet with our lives."

"I don't mean to interfere, Captain Aldebaran," said Mrs. Centauri. "But what's to stop the Grays from coming after Alan? Will he be safe on Earth?"

"I'm going to arrange for his protection," said my father.

"Actually, I might be able to help in that department, Atlas," said Senator Centauri. "The head of the Earthling Protection Agency is a close personal friend of mine. If I instruct him to, he'll put a 24-7 watch on your house in Kansas City. Just give me the address, and we'll make sure that no ship comes within 1000 miles of Alan while he's living on Earth."

"I'd welcome the assistance," said my father.

"Great, so not only am I going back to Earth tomorrow,

but I'm going to be spied on the whole time I'm there?" I said.

"Monitored," said my dad. "Protected."

I looked at him, incredulous, then slumped back in my chair. Senator Centauri put a hand on my shoulder.

"Orion, your father's right. Finish out your childhood on Earth. It'll be good for you. But just remember, as I said... you're an Aldebaran. You're meant to do great things."

My dad looked at him and said, "We're all meant to do great things," to which Mrs. Centauri nodded her agreement.

*　　*　　*　　*　　*

After dinner, Senator Centauri and my father retired to a private office to have some top secret political discussions, while Ari, Celeste and I went up to the roof deck and hung out beneath the stars, talking the night away. Actually, I shouldn't say all three of us, because within the first ten minutes, Ari fell asleep and started snoring, so it was really just me and Celeste making all the conversation. After waiting until Ari was lost in his dreams, muttering to himself and twitching, Celeste lowered her voice.

"So, pretty amazing," she said. "You saved your dad, defeated the Grays, and even got to kiss the girl."

"Huh?" I said, confused.

"I saw you kiss Jupiter Jones," said Celeste.

"She kissed me," I said.

"She'll be bragging about it at school tomorrow."

"Brag about kissing me? That'd be a first."

"Brag about kissing an Earthling," she said.

"Is that like a thing to do?" I said.

"Well, I don't know... It's kind of cool, isn't it?" she said, looking at me, "An intergalactic kiss."

Now, I'm sure it's as clear to you as it was to me that there was an opportunity here, a moment, but instead of seizing it, I just sat there paralyzed with fear, staring back at her like I'd been zapped with a freeze-ray. Luckily, Celeste was bold enough for the both of us and suddenly, out of the blue...

She kissed me. I was shocked. It was the second girl to plant one on me in 24 hours. She put one hand against the side of my cheek and the other behind my neck and pulled me towards her. Now, I told you from the first second I saw Celeste I was dumbstruck. I mean, she's cool, she's pretty, she's funny, she's smart and hey, she saved my life, which counts for a lot. And now, here she was, kissing me. I wasn't sure how it happened, where it came from, or where it was going, but I was enjoying every second of it...

And then, suddenly, Ari woke up.

"What time is it?" he said.

Celeste and I snapped apart and resumed our positions on the deck.

"I don't know. It's late," she said.

Ari stretched and groaned.

"Sorry, dude," he said. "I totally passed out. Hate to be a party-pooper on your last night in outer-space, but our little adventure has wiped me out."

"That's okay," I said.

"We should probably get some sleep," said Celeste.

"Yeah," I said.

We were all thinking the same thing — nobody wanted to say goodnight. But Ari, in his way, wasn't about to let the moment get too emotional.

"Come on, guys," he said. "Tomorrow isn't goodbye. It's just, 'see ya later'."

Chapter 11. ANDROMEDA ALDEBARAN

Ari may not have wanted a tearful goodbye, but that's pretty much what he got. He won't admit it now, but I could tell when we slapped hands and hugged for the last time, his eyes were a little glossy. Mine too.

One thing that eased the pain was the Intergalactic Transceiver. We were going to be able to keep in touch whenever we wanted, and Celeste made me promise to call as soon as I got settled in. I really wanted to ask her what our kiss meant, whether we were suddenly boyfriend and girlfriend or whether it was just some spur-of-the-moment Celeste thing that I shouldn't make too big a deal of, but I ultimately decided it was the second and kept my mouth shut.

My dad said his goodbyes to Polaris and Proxima Centauri and thanked them for taking such good care of us. Mrs. Centauri gave me a lunch bag filled with baked outer-space goodies and snacks for my trans-galactic flight, and that was that. With one last wave goodbye, my dad and I climbed into the belly of his spaceship and blasted off into space, leaving Alpha Centauri far below us.

The ride back to Earth was about four hours long and my dad and I talked almost the entire time. We talked about my ancestry, talked about my dad's most heroic missions in the armed forces, talked about Alpha Centauri politics and the evil intentions of The Grays and whether or not Earth would ever be invaded. But mostly, we talked about my mother, Andromeda Aldebaran.

"Your mom was an Earthling, just like you. She was born on Earth, whereas I was born in space," began my dad.

"Then how did you meet?" I said.

"At the movies, like we've always told you. The only difference is, I came from a lot further away than 'the other side of town.' When I was young, a lot of teenagers from Alpha Centauri would make intergalactic jaunts to Earth. That's how we'd get our kicks. It was dangerous, but it was fun. And there was no E.P.A. back then to stop you."

"My friends and I came down to see a movie. We loved movies, and the best ones came from Earth. We saw Star Wars. It was 1977. And I met your mother at the Stratford Theater in Kansas City, on June 15th. We fell in love at first sight. And I proceeded to come back to Earth and visit her every chance I got."

He grinned, reminiscing.

"Of course, I wasn't sure how to tell her I was from outer space. I tried once and she thought it was a big practical joke, so I just played along. I wound up having to lie to her, which I hated. I told her that I was in the United States military and that I was always being sent to different countries around the world. And that's how our relationship stayed, for almost a year."

"And then, one day, I just went for it. I revealed the truth. I showed your mom my spaceship and took her into outer space. I let her see everything, and I introduced her to everyone. Now that was something you just weren't supposed to do. Well, you can only imagine how stunned she was. I mean, there are probably only a few hundred Earthlings who have actually been to other planets, and as you know, it's a big shock to the system. But you know what happened?"

I shook my head.

"Your mother fit in immediately. I mean, everyone who met her, loved her. All my friends and family. Nobody cared she was from Earth. In fact, within a few months, people were suggesting that she run for political office, even though she was an Earthling. She inspired people. And that's when I knew I wanted to marry her. I proposed and two months later we got married in the Orion Nebula, in the Trapezium. That's how we came up with your name. It was a beautiful ceremony under the quadruple suns."

"After that, your mother went back to Earth to finish out college, and I stayed in space and joined the military. Of course we saw each other all the time. But it was a hard period in our lives, a lot of traveling."

"If she's from Earth, how did she get the name Andromeda?"

"That's a name that she was given when she married into my family. She decided she would use Andromeda as her name in outer space, and on Earth, she was Karen. "

I was fascinated. But there was still one thing I wanted to know most of all and so finally I asked him, point blank:

"How did she die, dad?"

My father went silent for a long time. When he finally spoke, his voice was shaking.

"I'm ashamed to tell you this story, but I'm going to, because I promised I'd never hide anything from you again..."

"After your mother and I were abducted, we were taken to The Gray Planet. You know that already. The Grays, they kept us separated, locked up in different jail cells. I didn't see your mother for 3 straight months. I couldn't bear not knowing what was happening to her. Every day I begged and pleaded with The Gray Queen to let your mother go."

I could hear a mix of anger and regret building in his voice.

"Finally, one day, out of the blue, The Gray Queen agreed. She told me she was sending your mother back to Earth. And for some reason, I believed her."

"A few days later, I was in my prison cell, and I overheard a conversation between The Gray Queen and her military commanders. They were describing their plans to invade Earth. I heard them talk about a ship that was carrying a plasma bomb, a device one thousand times more destructive than the most powerful weapon on Earth."

My eyes went wide.

"They were going to drop a bomb on Earth?"

My dad nodded.

"I heard the whole battle-plan through the ventilation ducts. I carefully recorded every single detail of the plan, including the identification number of the ship. Then, I managed to escape my cell and I contacted the League of Planets, relaying everything I heard over an intergalactic radio. I was eventually recaptured by The Grays and thrown back in jail. But I had succeeded. I had gotten the information out. And within days, the League of Planets tracked down the Gray ship I identified and blew it out of the stars."

He paused, swallowing back tears.

"Only, there was no bomb, Alan. There was no plan to attack Earth at all. The ship we blew up was the one carrying your mother back home to Missouri."

My heart sank.

"They Gray Queen set me up. She arranged it so that I was responsible for your mother's death. And I have to live with that every day of my life."

I sat there in stunned silence.

"I'm sorry, dad," I said.

"So am I," he said.

*   *   *   *   *

I guess my alien adventure finally caught up with me, because somewhere in the middle of my dad's stories, I fell asleep. An hour later, he gently shook my shoulder.

"Have a nice nap?" he said.

I woke up, a little groggy.

"Take a look."

As I came to, I peered out the front windshield of our ship to see the most beautiful sight I'd ever seen: Planet Earth, in all her blue and green majesty, a perfectly round marble, floating in space.

"We're home," he said.

I couldn't believe I had slept so long. I missed the entire trip through the Solar System, which kind of stunk, because I really wanted to see the rings of Saturn again.

As we approached Earth, my father pressed a button on his ship's console and sent a transmission to the Earthling Protection Agency, identifying himself as Atlas Aldebaran. He gave a security clearance code, which, when processed, caused the E.P.A. to suddenly react with nothing but the utmost respect, even awe.

"Yes, sir, Captain Aldebaran, you are cleared for passage. If we can be of any assistance on your visit to Earth, please let us know."

"Thank you," said my dad.

We descended into the atmosphere, then down through the bumpy sub-stratosphere, until we reached airplane altitude, about 20,000 feet up. We made our way around the globe, zooming over the continents, until we started descending over America. I asked my dad if there was any danger of being picked up on some military radar, like a true unidentified Flying Object, but he assured me the cloaking technology on his ship was top-of-the line and undetectable to Earthling radar. The only real issue was if we were seen with the naked eye. But we all know how people reporting UFO sightings are treated on Earth and so really there was no danger at all.

Finally, within a few minutes, we reached Missouri. My dad pushed downward on the ship's controls and we made our descent. I began to recognize the familiar landscape of my home state. The wide-open crop fields and thick, sprawling forests were a welcome sight. I was back. I was home. And I was thrilled.

But then something weird happened. As we saw our family barn approaching, my dad simply kept flying, right over our property, steering us into the forest that surrounds our backyard. With perfect control, he went soaring over the trees, found a gap in the forest canopy, and then dove down into the middle of the woods. He touched down on the forest floor with a perfect landing and then shut off the ship, looking over at me. I could tell immediately something was wrong.

"What is it?" I asked.

My dad was silent for a long time.

"I'm not staying," he said.

"What?"

"I'm going back into space. To find out who betrayed us and avenge your mother's death. It's my duty."

"But we need you here, me and Katie..."

"Alan, listen to me — There's a conspiracy going on, between The Grays and some of the politicians in the League of Planets."

"What?" I said, my mind suddenly switching gears, "What conspiracy?"

"Politicians I thought I could trust are secretly working with the Grays to help them destroy Earth. It's these same people who sold me out, who gave the Grays the money and the intelligence to build the black hole generator... It's these people, Alan, who are responsible for your mother's death. I have to find out who they are and bring them to justice."

I didn't know what to say. I wanted to feel angry with my father for leaving me again, but instead, I only felt one thing: I wanted to go with him.

"Take me with you," I said.

He shook his head.

"It's too dangerous."

"But... what about Katie?" I said, trying to think of anything to make him change his mind. "What am I supposed to tell her?"

"Tell her everything. I don't want any more secrets, Alan. And also tell her, once I've done my duty, I'll be back for both of you."

He put a hand on my shoulder.

"You're going to be okay. I know that now. Remember, you rescued _me_," he said, grinning. "You're not just Alan Albright. You're also Orion Aldebaran. I'm proud of you, son."

"No, dad, I don't want you to go... not yet. At least stay until—"

He shook his head, then reached forward and pulled me close. I held on to him tightly because I knew the second that we stopped hugging, he was going to leave and I would lose that feeling I had enjoyed for the last 24 hours, a feeling of safety and warmth that I wanted to hold on to. I just sat there, and he let me, and we hugged for a good five minutes until finally the sun went down.

"I love you, Alan," said my dad.

"I love you, too," I said.

He pulled back and kissed me on the forehead. I unbuckled my seat belt and opened the passenger door and climbed down the ladder, setting foot on Planet Earth for the first time in what seemed like forever.

As my dad turned on the ignition, I felt tempted to shout something, anything to extend the moment just a second longer. But before I could think of what to say, his ship roared to life and went blasting off through the trees and I was alone.

I took a deep breath and wiped the tears from my face. I turned around. I knew exactly where I was -- not even five minutes from my house. The moment that sunk in, the despair of saying goodbye to my father turned into utter exhilaration, and I broke out into a sprint.

I don't think I ever ran so fast in my life, down a forest path, whisks of branches whipping me in the face. I took huge jumps over fallen logs and even did a graceful leap across the creek that separates the edge of the forest from our property. I felt like a pro athlete, going on pure adrenaline, and before I knew it, I was home.

I saw a light on in the kitchen window and I could

hear the ever-so-faint sound of conversation. It was around six o'clock on Monday night, which meant they were probably just finishing up family dinner and were about to start one of grandmom's amazing desserts.

I quickly patted my hair down, caught my breath and made my way to the front porch. My heart was pounding in my chest, and even though I knew this was going to be a pretty serious moment, I just couldn't get the smile off my face. I was beaming. My cheeks were practically up at my ears. I knew I'd have a lot of explaining to do. I knew my grandparents and Katie were probably worried sick about me for the last two days. But we'd address all of that later. I wasn't thinking about that. I was thinking about the initial moment when I walked through the door and caught them all by surprise—

"Alan?" said my sister.

I stopped short. Katie was standing behind the screen door, peering out at me with wide eyes.

"Alan!" she screamed. "Mom-mom, GrandPop! He's home!"

And then, my little sister, who I've had so many fights with I can't even count them, came bursting out the front door, ran down our porch steps and jumped into my arms. I found myself squeezing her in the tightest hug we have ever and probably will ever share. It was so emotional that I lost my balance and toppled over and Katie and I went crashing onto the front lawn, laughing.

"Are you okay?" she kept repeating. "Please tell me you're okay!"

"I'm okay, Katie," I said.

My grandparents suddenly appeared on the porch behind us. The minute my grandmother saw me, she got faint and her legs get wobbly and she started tipping over. Grandpop moved quickly to grab her, and together they descended the stairs as fast as I've ever seen them move. They joined me and Katie and we all hugged for a long, long time.

"What happened to you, Alan?" my grandfather said through tears.

After warning them that they weren't going to believe a single word of it, we went inside, sat down at the kitchen table, and I began to tell them the whole incredible story.

Chapter 12. REASSIMILATING TO LIFE ON EARTH

Well, as you might have guessed, the 'whole incredible story' didn't go over too well. As I gobbled down warm apple pie and a glass of cold milk, I did my best to explain the improbable series of events I had just been through. My dad had given me the green light to tell as much of the story as I wanted, and I decided to tell it all.

Of course, I didn't really expect my family to believe me right away, but I certainly didn't think they'd be as upset as they were either. My grandparents' overall reaction was that I was having an emotional breakdown, and that I had made the whole story up as some kind of escapist fantasy, as a means of dealing with the death of my parents.

So, the very next morning, they took me downtown to see a child psychologist. I was forced to explain the entire course of events all over, only this time to some doctor, while lying on a couch. She kept trying to find flaws in my abduction tale to prove I had made it up, and I just kept giving her more and more details, all of which fit together like a jigsaw puzzle. By the time our session had ended, I think the psychologist was the one who was a little crazy.

In any case, it didn't really matter much. My

grandparents were just glad to have me back home safe and sound and were quick to let the whole incident slide so long as I promised never to 'run away' again.

Katie, on the other hand, found my story very interesting and continually asked me little details about it here and there, like what did our dad look like and how did he act and was he happy and so on. She absolutely loved it when I told her her outer space name was Aurora and she started making me call her by it all the time. I didn't really think she believed everything I was saying, in fact, I'm sure she didn't, but I think talking about "Atlas and Andromeda Aldebaran" was kind of like therapy for her and in a weird way it brought us closer together.

I also told Andy everything that happened and as I expected he believed every single word. He never doubted my story and after all I'd been through it was sure nice to have at least one person on Earth who took me 100% seriously. He became obsessed with the data and information I had about aliens, like who were The Grays, what did Lyrians look like and how many types of humans were there. He even started posting the info I gave him at andyweinerblogspot.com, so you can go there and read what he's been writing if you want.

*   *   *   *   *

Then, when school started in September, something very strange happened — for the first time in my life, I got good grades. I mean really good grades. Maybe it was because I was happier, or because I finally learned the truth about my parents, but it was so much easier to pay attention in class. I could recall everything, like I had a photographic memory. I got straight A's on every single exam and quiz for the first month of the year, in every single class. And because I went from C's to A's faster than any kid in the school's history, I really raised some eyebrows.

It all came to a head after a particularly astonishing A+ on the hardest pop quiz of my life, when Mrs. Peachtree instructed me to stay after class — for cheating.

"How else do you explain the miraculous turn around in your school work?" she said.

"I don't know, Mrs. Peachtree. I've just changed. I can't explain it..."

"Alan, no offense, but last year you were a C student, at best. The things you're doing in your homework, and on your tests, well, frankly, their indicative of much higher intelligence than you've ever displayed before."

"Okay...?" I said.

"What do you expect me to make of this?"

"I don't know. But it's not cheating. Don't you know me better than that?"

She studied me.

"It's true," she said. "You've worked hard for me in the tutoring program. You're a good kid. And it would be awfully hard to cheat so often, so successfully, without getting caught. So you're telling me the absolute truth?"

"I guess I'm just smarter this year," I said.

"Well then I'm going to bump you up to honors English. Until you prove otherwise, you're up for much bigger challenges than I'm offering here."

And that's how I wound up in Mrs. Peachtree's Honors English class, and that's how this journal came about. The assignments in the H-track classes are a little more creative and last week Mrs. Peachtree simply handed us these composition books with one single instruction: "Fill them." She didn't give us a specific due date, just that they had to be turned in sometime by the end of the school year and that we could write about whatever we wanted. I took the assignment as the perfect opportunity to start documenting my adventure and so for the last few days I've been scrawling away, writing these pages at light-speed. And although my hand is killing me, I feel very satisfied with what I've written here. This is an honest and accurate account of my alien abduction. My plan now is to set it aside, re-read it a few times, and then probably hand it in sometime around winter break. If anything else interesting happens to me between now and then, I'll make sure to write about it. But otherwise, I have a feeling that my life here on Earth has finally returned to normal. And I plan to enjoy it.

CHAPTER 13. UNCLE AJAX

Well, that didn't last long. It hasn't been a week since I wrote that last sentence and something has happened that I need to tell you about. In fact, the story's not complete without this, the final chapter, an account of what happened this very night, Saturday November 1st, 2008.

It all started at around 10 o'clock, when I went out to the barn to call Celeste on the Intergalactic Transceiver. We'd been doing this every Saturday night since I'd returned to Earth, kind of like dates, the two of us chatting about everything and anything under the stars. We probably had the longest-long-distance relationship in the known universe, although I still wasn't sure if we were actually boyfriend and girlfriend.

After I faked saying goodnight to my grandparents and Katie, I slipped outside the house and made my way across the fields, past the animal pens, to the barn. The sky was rumbling with the sound of distant thunder and lightning was popping like flashbulbs behind the gathering clouds. I figured the storm would be on us in about an hour and made a mental note to keep my conversation with Celeste short since the barn leaked and I didn't want to get stuck out there in the rain.

Peanut Butter and Jelly were already asleep in their stables and so I tried to be as quiet as possible as I climbed the ladder to the 3rd floor. Much to my surprise, as I poked my head through the hatch, I could already hear Celeste's voice coming out of the Intergalactic Transceiver.

"Alan, where are you?" she said. "Pick up, pick up..."

I reached the microphone and clicked it on.

"Hello?

"Alan, good, you're there. We have to talk."

I'm embarrassed to say it, but I thought she was referring to our relationship.

"Yeah, I agree," I said.

"You do?"

"Yeah," I said. "Look, Celeste, I'm just going to come out with it. I like you. I mean it's pretty obvious. And I know we're light-years apart but—"

"Alan, no, that's not it," she said, and I felt my face go red, which was weird since I was alone.

"It's about my father," she continued.

"What about him?" I said.

She went silent for a long time.

"Celeste—?"

"Alan, I don't know how to say this, but I think my dad might be working with The Grays."

She had caught me totally off-guard.

"What?"

"I don't want to believe it, and I probably should wait to find out more proof, but I decided to say something because they might be coming for you."

"Who?"

"The Grays," she said.

"Coming here?" I said. I couldn't believe what she was telling me. "How do you know all this, Celeste?"

"I overheard my dad," she said. "He was talking on the phone and I was... eavesdropping... and now I just wish I hadn't heard anything. But he said your name... and Katie's... and that you're both going to be abducted."

"Katie?" I said.

"Yes..."

My brain went into overdrive.

"When?"

"I don't know. But I think they're watching your house. They may even be listening to this call."

A sudden chill went through me and I glanced out the

barn window.

"What about the Earthling Protection Agency?" I said.

"They're in on it," she said.

I was floored.

"Celeste... what are you telling me?"

"It's a conspiracy, Alan, to bring down your family once and for all," said Celeste. "And I think my dad's involved."

Part of me wanted to shut the radio off. I didn't want to hear anymore, because every word out of Celeste's mouth was making me more and more scared.

"I have to get in touch with my father," I said.

"How?" she said. "Nobody knows where he is."

She was right, of course. But before I could even stop and figure out my next move, I suddenly noticed some strange lights flickering outside the window. I peered into the navy blue sky and saw something twinkling in the distance, drawing closer. I still had the CB in my hand, stretching the corkscrew cord into a taut line as I peered out the window.

"Celeste...?" I said.

"I'm here," she said.

"I think there's something out there," I said.

"Where?"

"In the sky... above my farm." I narrowed my gaze, squinting. "I think it's a ship."

"Alan! Run!"

No sooner did Celeste get the words out than a blinding beam of white light came bursting through the 3rd floor window. Above me, I heard a strange vibration and a loud ripping sound and then... vwoosh... the roof of the barn was torn off, like a giant hand had grabbed it and pried it loose. Wooden planks went flying as the beam started sweeping around the area, like a spotlight. And then, as I peered up, I saw it... an enormous silver UFO spinning right above my barn. The Grays had come for me.

I dove across the floor, landing in a pile of haystacks. The planks came raining down around me as I rolled towards a trough and pulled it over my head. It was like being in a coffin or a tomb. I heard pieces of wood smacking down above me, but I remained safe inside. Finally, all sound stopped. I gathered my courage and lifted the edge of the trough...

The entire 3rd floor of the barn was gone, leaving nothing but a skeleton frame of crossbeams. I stared up into the star-filled night, scanning the sky, eyes wide.

Suddenly I saw the ship in the distance, a black shadow coming back around —

I grabbed the ladder and slid down to the 2nd floor, and then, this I've done many times, I jumped from the 2nd floor to the first, doing a rolling-landing in the hay. I ran to the indoor stables and found Peanut Butter and leapt onto his back, waking him up. He whinnied and stood up on all fours, confused.

"Hiya!" I said, snapping the reigns.

Peanut Butter came to life and went galloping out of the barn like a thunderbolt. The Gray UFO appeared above us, firing a rapid-stream of blue lasers that I instantly recognized as freeze-rays, confirming that they were here to abduct me, not kill me... but that didn't make me feel any better. Peanut Butter cut left and right, creating big divots in the Earth as blue laser beams peppered the landscape behind us. He leapt over a log and kept up full throttle until suddenly...

The attack stopped. The ship went silent. And then, right before my very eyes it disappeared. It was like watching the Justice League cartoons when Wonder Woman made her jet turn invisible. I mean, it just vanished. I brought Peanut Butter to a halt, confused for a moment.

And then I realized --

"Katie!"

I snapped the reigns again and off we went, making a beeline straight for the house, Peanut Butter going the fastest he's ever gone. I scanned the sky but I couldn't see the ship anywhere. We reached the back porch and I leapt from the saddle and hit the ground running. I didn't even stop to tie Peanut Butter to a rail, just darted up the steps, grabbed the sliding glass kitchen door and yanked it open.

Everything was eerily still inside the house. I heard the sound of our TV playing a Saturday evening local news show. As I tiptoed into the living room, I grabbed a metal iron poker from beside the fireplace and slowly moved toward the double-recliners in the den, where I could make out the backs of my grandparents' heads, each in their respective comfy chair.

"Grandma?" I said. "Grandpa?"

Neither of them responded. I inched closer... and then I realized something was wrong. They were being too still. As I reached them, I saw the side of my grandfather's face bathed in the pale light of the television broadcast. I realized he wasn't asleep -- his eyes were open, but they weren't blinking. I reached out and put a hand on his recliner, rotating him towards me. And there, in one of the creepiest moments of my entire life, I saw my grandfather's motionless body, frozen in the chair like he was a wax statue.

I glanced at my grandmother beside him. She was frozen stiff, too. I nudged her and she didn't respond and suddenly it hit me... they'd been zapped with a freeze-ray. And that could only mean one thing... The Grays were inside the house.

Suddenly, I heard a scream.

"HEEEELP!!!

It was Katie.

Every muscle in my body sprang to life and I was on the stairs, taking two at a time, gripping the fire poker, white-knuckled.

I made it upstairs and bounded down the hallway to Katie's room. The door was closed but I didn't even hesitate, leaping forward and kicking it open, pretty sure that the puny lock would give. The door flew open so hard that it almost broke off the hinges.

There, across the room, I saw Katie getting wrestled toward the window by a Gray.

"Alan!" she screamed.

The Gray suddenly turned toward me, but I didn't even give him time to react — I just ran through the room and swung the iron poker at his head, doing my best Babe Ruth impersonation.

WHAM! I caught the Gray square in the side of his face. There was a sickening thwack followed by a pained scream as he dropped my sister and fell to the floor, writhing.

"Katie, get out of here!"

She just stood there, staring at the alien, as shocked as I had been the first time I saw one. I knew there was no way she was going to come to her senses and run, so I grabbed her hand and together we went bolting from the room.

We ran downstairs and I lead her across the kitchen to the back screen door.

"What about Grandma and Grandpa?!" she screamed.

"They're here for us, not them," I said, pushing on the handle, flinging open the door. We scrambled down the porch steps where Peanut Butter was still waiting. I practically jumped into the saddle, placing my foot into his stirrup and swinging my leg over until I was sitting tight. Then I reached down and grabbed Katie, nearly yanking her arm out of the socket as I pulled her up. She straddled the horse behind me, arms around my waist.

I snapped the reigns and Peanut Butter took off like lightning again. Suddenly the massive UFO appeared above us and started firing. All around us, the night was getting lit up like a planetarium show, blue lasers cutting through the air. The beams were missing us by inches and I knew it was only a matter of time before we got hit...

"Jump!" I screamed.

I grabbed Katie and pulled her out of the saddle, just as a laser-beam zapped Peanut Butter right in the chest. We fell to the ground and went rolling into the cropfields, cushioned by the stalks of corn, watching in complete horror as our horse got frozen in mid-gallop and tipped over. Katie started to scream but I clamped my hand over her mouth and kept her silent as we crouched there, hiding.

Suddenly, the silver UFO descended, landing in the middle of our fields. A ramp lowered, a light came bursting out and the silhouettes of four Grays appeared. They strode down the ramp, disappearing into the cornfields around us.

I looked over at my sister. She was practically

shaking with fear.

"Go to Andy's house. You understand me? Don't stop for anything."

"What about you?" she said.

"I'm going to distract them until I'm sure you're safe. Then I'll meet you there."

"No, Alan... It's too dangerous!"

"This is our farm, Katie. We know it better than anyone. How many times have we played hide and seek in these fields?"

"A million," she said.

"That's right. We can outfox these guys. Now get to Andy's house... he knows everything. I'll be right behind you."

Suddenly, laser beams came flying overhead.

"Go!" I said.

Katie took one last look at me then turned and disappeared into the tall stalks. I started running in the opposite direction, drawing their fire away from her. I cut this way and that, making my way across the farm. I had an idea. If I could get to the wheat fields, it would be waiting there for me...

And there it was. My father's favorite vehicle on Earth, the John Deere 5025 series tractor, with a giant scoop-plow up front and crane-claw in back. Like I mentioned earlier, running the farm had fallen squarely on my shoulders and I'd become proficient at handling all our heavy machinery... including this monster.

I scaled the ladder and climbed into the cushioned cab. The key was in the glove compartment and just as The Grays emerged from the cornfields, I removed it, stuck it in the ignition and turned over the engine. I pulled a lever and raised the scoop, then pushed on the gas and powered forward. The Grays were shocked, drawing their laser guns... but I was faster. I flipped on the tractor's headlights and blinded them, then drove forward and scooped two of them right up, lifting them high into the air. I rotated the tractor and dumped them into the cornfields, burying them in a pile of dirt.

Their comrades had dodged out of the way, and were now firing lasers at me from behind. I rotated the rear crane, whipping it around like a demolition ball, hitting one of them square in the side. He went flying through the air, landing face-first into the dirt.

But I had lost sight of the other one. And when the

cab started exploding with sparks and smoke, I knew he'd gotten the drop on me. I looked out the rear view mirror to see him running right toward me, squeezing off a stream of freeze-rays.

I slammed on the gas, crushing cornstalks beneath the tractor's immense wheels as the alien chased me on foot. Tractors can reach pretty fast speeds and I was easily putting some distance between us, but the interior of the cab was thick with smoke and a small fire had erupted on the dashboard. I had no choice. I had to get out.

I kicked open the door and dove out of the tractor, hitting the ground, hard. As I lay there, wheezing, I suddenly saw the Gray alien coming up right behind me, illuminated in the moonlight. He seemed to glow-in-the-dark, sending chills down my spine. Even though I could barely breathe, I climbed to my feet and took off running again, emerging into the large barnyard that served as our backyard.

I ran for the cow pen and dove right in, landing amid the herd. The Gray appeared at the fence and started firing freeze-rays at me as I crawled among the cows. Some of them got hit and became instantly motionless, like someone had paused them, their moos getting cut short. The rest of the herd started to panic, cowering away, nearly trampling me as I crawled on my hands and knees across the pen.

I reached the gate on the far side and noticed a lasso hanging there. I took the rope down and crept out of the pen, then snuck up on The Gray as he kept firing his lasers into the herd, having lost sight of me. Ever so quietly, I twirled the lasso overhead and flicked my wrist, tossing the rope toward the alien. He noticed it at the last second and turned toward me, raising his laser-gun.

But he was too late. The rope encircled his shoulders and I yanked it tight, ensnaring him. His arms went flat at his sides and I pulled until he was squeezed so hard that the gun dropped from his fingers. I jerked the rope and he fell to the ground.

I walked over and wrapped him around a few more times and then, when I was sure he was secure, I reached down and picked up his freeze-ray. No sooner did I have it in my hands when --

"Release your weapon."

I looked back to see another Gray standing behind me, one hand on his gun, the other holding my sister around her neck. I whirled around, aiming at him.

"Let her go!" I said.

"I'm sorry, Alan. I tried to get away..."

"Katie, you did nothing wrong. Everything's going to be okay," I said.

"Drop the weapon or your sister dies," said the Gray.

I looked at him for a long time, staring into his oval black eyes.

"I don't think so," I finally said. "I think you were sent to capture us, not kill us. That's why you're only using freeze-rays."

He went quiet.

"Which means, what we have is a stalemate," I went on, trying to sound brave. "Now, I know you can't disappoint your Queen, so why don't we make a deal? Let my sister go, and I'll surrender myself to you without a fight."

"No!" said Katie.

The Gray studied me.

"Well?" I said. "Do we have a deal?"

"You're right about one thing," said the Gray. "I can't disappoint my Queen."

Suddenly, he aimed his weapon at me and fired...

What followed seemed to happen in slow motion — The laser beam left his gun and cut a path straight towards me.

My eyes widened and my mind seemed to stand still, but somehow, my body knew just what to do and I dropped to the ground, rolling under the blue laser as it sizzled overhead. In one fluid movement, I took to my knee and aimed the freeze-ray.

"Katie, get down!"

She dropped to her belly in the mud and I squeezed the trigger. A blue laser sliced through the air and hit The Gray smack in the center of the chest. His features and body froze in time, like he was a statue, and then he tipped over and hit the Earth with a thud, immobile.

Katie climbed to her feet and ran to me, as the skies overhead finally ripped open, dropping buckets of rain across the farm. We stood there embracing when suddenly we heard a loud humming noise and the massive Gray spaceship appeared again, lights twinkling. Only this time, it wasn't coming for us — One by one, it picked up the fallen Grays using the tractor beam, levitating them into the belly of the ship.

It hovered high above the farm for a moment, as if to say 'we'll be back', before finally speeding off into the night. Katie looked up at me, tears running down her face.

"I'm sorry I messed everything up," she said.

"Are you kidding? You were amazing!" I said. "Mom and dad would be proud of you, Katie."

She smiled through her tears and we stood there hugging each other for a minute, when suddenly, her eyes narrowed and she pulled away.

"What's wrong?" I said.

Katie stared off into the night sky.

"They're coming back," she said.

I turned around, peering through the rain. Three twinkling lights were coming right towards us. I was about to grab Katie's hand and run, but then I realized that something was off. It wasn't the Grays. This ship looked like a small jet, with a long nose and two little wings.

It angled toward our farm, slightly out of control. Katie and I craned our necks and watched as it soared overhead and then touched down with a bumpy landing. There was a hiss of pressurized air and then a hatch opened and a man climbed out wearing a flight-suit and brandishing a laser gun.

On first glance, this man looked so much like my father that Katie even said, "Dad?" and ran toward him. But then she stopped and did a double-take, because there was something slightly different about his features. He was maybe 5 years older than my father and a little heavier, with a bushy beard.

I walked forward and stood beside Katie.

"You're not our father," I said.

The man shook his head.

"No," he said. "I'm your Uncle. Ajax."

"We have an Uncle Ajax?" said Katie, looking at me.

"Your father entrusted me with your safety and I'm sorry to say, I let him down. I didn't get tipped off about what The Grays were up to until it was too late. But I came immediately... Are either of you hurt?" he said.

"No, we're fine," said Katie. "Alan saved us."

"You fended them off yourself?" asked Uncle Ajax.

I nodded and he roared with laughter at this, clasping a beefy hand on my shoulder.

"That's twice you've gotten the best of The Grays!" said Ajax. "I've heard some pretty impressive stories about you already, young Orion. You're shaping up to be much more the hero than your father was at your age."

He clapped his hands together.

"Well, then, I'm glad you're both safe. Let's gather up your things. I want to be off this planet in five minutes."

Katie and I stopped short and looked at each other, then at him.

"What are you talking about?" I said.

"Well surely you can't stay here anymore," said Ajax. "The Grays have more friends and allies than we ever suspected. There's no doubt in my mind they'll try to abduct you both again. Maybe even tonight."

"So you want us to leave Earth with you, right now?" I said.

"Forever?" said Katie.

"Your father asked me to keep you both safe while he handles some personal business. Our arrangement was, if you should come into any danger, I'm to take you back to Alpha Centauri with me until he returns."

He paused, then added —

"After all, I'm your godfather."

"But I don't want to leave..." said Katie.

My uncle looked at her and was about to say something, but instead glanced over at me, as if to say, 'You convince her'. But honestly, I wasn't sure I was ready for this either. The odds were, if we got into that ship with our uncle Ajax, we might never set foot on planet Earth again. We were being asked to say goodbye to our entire life in Kansas City.

But The Grays were getting more aggressive. And staying on Earth would almost certainly mean putting Katie and my grandparents in danger. And since I couldn't live with myself if something ever happened to them, I knew what I had to do.

"It's going to be okay, Katie," I said, kneeling down to her. "We'll be together. We'll be safe."

She looked at me in a way she never had before, like she believed in me.

"What about mom-mom and grandpop?" she said.

"Where are they?" said Ajax.

"Inside," I said. "They got hit with a freeze-ray."

"Well, they'll be fine. It wears off in a few hours," said Ajax.

"How will they know what happened to us?" said Katie.

"Leave them a note," said Ajax.

I thought it through.

"That's exactly what we're going to do," I said. "Only I need more than five minutes to write it."

I convinced Ajax that since I'd spent so much time already on this journal, he should let me have one more hour to add this last chapter. And so that's where I am now, holed up in my room, writing as fast as possible while hoping against hope that some more Grays don't show up and abduct me before I finish this sentence. Katie is in her room deciding which dolls are worthy of space travel and which should stay behind on Earth. If all goes according to plan, in a few minutes, the two of us are going to go blasting off in Uncle Ajax's ship. And even though I feel terrible about how all this will affect my grandparents, I gotta admit, I'm super excited to go back into outer space again.

It's time to finish this journal now, once and for all. I'm going to leave it on the kitchen table and hopefully it'll serve as our goodbye note. Although, the truth is, anybody who reads it will probably think I made all this up anyway. It's just too hard to believe that there's a whole universe of intelligent life in outer space that people on Earth know nothing about. All I can say to that is what my dad used to say to me...

Sometimes the truth is stranger than fiction.